THE LAST LOT WITH A VIEW
The Life of Larry and Ann Horton

A Biographical Novel
By Kristopher Horton

FIRST EDITION

ISBN: 978-01542932820

ACKNOWLEDGEMENTS

As with any book, it's practically impossible to put together a complete work without the help of a multitude of people. It all started with Ann and Larry Horton who were both extremely gracious and poignant through several dozen interviews. They shared the highs and lows of their lives both together and apart, giving not only examples of their personal beliefs and successes, but also glimpses into their vulnerabilities.

Their five sons, Craig, Stan, Steve, Chuck, and Jerry, added details and an additional perspective to the narrative. Beyond interviews, Dawna Curler's well researched and wonderfully written, *Always Do the Right Thing: The One Hundred Year Legacy of Lawrence's Jewelers*, provided insights into the family business.

My thanks go to those who helped me polish this collection of family stories, most notable, my editor, Luke Nelson whose keen editorial prowess honed and focused the narrative. A very special thanks to my wife, Marian, whose support and love were instrumental in completing the book.

While this work started as a biography, it quickly became seduced to the realm of biographical novel by the compelling nature of Ann and Larry's storied lives. To that extent, this is closer to a memoirs than a book of historical fact. Very often primary sources remember things differently and the intention of the narrative is to remain accurate to Ann and Larry's interpretation of events.

Bringing the past to life was no easy task! Dialog presented a unique challenge, as other than some examples of dialog from letters or Larry's previous writings, very little actual dialog was preserved. To allow people to speak in their own voices, a technique was utilized where words from modern day interviews would be transposed to fit the historic setting. For example, in an interview, Larry said, "I had a decision to make, she had a decision to make..." which became "You have a decision to make, I have a decision to make...." So while much of the dialog likely did not occur the way it is written, it does reflect people's memories of the events. This use of 'presentism' further distorts the historic lens, as modern sensibilities and interpretations are applied to the events of the past.

In short, this book is 'based on actual events.' It gives a glimpse into the lives of Ann and Larry Horton, showing the forces that shaped their destinies and how hard work, determination, and a vision for the future earned them the American Dream.

THE LAST LOT WITH A VIEW

1

Paradise Lost
Medford, Oregon 1964

Larry Horton's social contacts competed to be the matchmaker to introduce this recent widower to his next wife. He met with a nurse, pianist, secretary, homemaker, and now Larry stood under the glowing, pink neon sign for Lawrence's Jewelers.

The sun was out and only faint wisps of his breath puffed around his cheeks. Through the rounded window he watched a woman wrap a box in silvery paper. A year prior and he would have been buying a Christmas present for his deceased wife.

Inside the store, he introduced himself and waited for Ann. When she emerged from the walk-in safe, Larry was momentarily speechless. He'd seen her before in the local paper, advertising for cutlery, watches, china, or any number of things the store sold, but that was a portrait in grainy black and white and this was his first glimpse of her filled with the vibrance of life. She was attired like a woman from the Bloomingdales catalog in a dress that shimmered under halogen lights, accentuated with a mix of gold and gemstone jewelry, and her blonde up-styled hair. He had never seen anyone like her before.

They walked a few short blocks to the Colony Far East, a restaurant that served Americanized Chinese food: Sweet and Sour Pork, Fried Rice, and of course, Mar Far Chicken, a dish that had been invented and popularized by their rival Southern Oregon establishment, Kim's Chinese Cuisine. Larry suggested the restaurant because of its proximity to the jewelry store and because he had been there before for lunch meetings. But that had been Larry eating in the company of business associates, men and women collaborating on engineering and civic projects. This was his first time with a woman who dazzled him. They ordered, neither paying much attention to the menu, or the food.

"Bob Balk tells me you have a J. Henry Helsner account," Larry said.

"Has anyone talked to Bob and not ended up with an investment account?" Ann laughed, revealing her perfect gleaming teeth.

"I talked to Bob and ended up with a date."

"Yes, you did." Ann smiled.

Larry had always been shy. After several years in Kiwanis and Toastmasters, he mastered public speaking, but he couldn't match Ann's natural grace and friendliness. Watching her now left Larry yearning for more smiles and laughter. He attempted the cleverness of fathers and businessmen; it fell short of flirtation. When smiles and laughs did not follow, he changed to safe topics.

"Do you live around here?" he asked. Medford was growing, but most people still lived near the city center.

"Highland and Barneburg."

"I'm just around the corner on Barneburg."

"It's a small world." Ann laughed again.

Surprisingly they hadn't even glimpsed one another before today. They were both members of service organizations, however, prior to the eighties, men and women predominantly belonged to gender-exclusive clubs. Larry belonged to Kiwanis, and Ann to Zonta. They both had teenage boys of similar age: Larry's youngest and Ann's oldest attended the same junior high.

However, Larry was still recovering from the death of his wife, Marty. While he approached re-marriage like an electrical engineer evaluating voltage requirements, on a subconscious level he was looking for a dedicated homemaker. Ann had been a working single-mother for over a decade. Larry didn't know what to make of that as he didn't know any single women who worked to support their families.

Larry's marital dilemma was far from resolved.

Larry habitually countered difficulty with determined forward progress. The trait was a defining characteristic of Larry's success in engineering, one that gave him the strength to recover from losing a job by starting a consulting business. Now it provided him with impetus to get his boys out of the house by taking them on a road trip to Pasadena, California to watch his alma matter, Oregon State, compete in the 51st Rose Bowl. They stayed with Larry's younger brother, Dean.

In an unexpected twist, an old family friend, Shirley, had recently divorced and was planning a move from Los Angeles back to the Rogue Valley. Larry met her for a dinner date. They indulged in remembrances of mutual friends and shared experiences. It was a familiar comfort

Larry missed since Marty's passing.

But the boys wouldn't let him forget the real reason for the trip. They skipped the 75th annual Rose Parade and went straight to the stadium. The Oregon State Beavers scored early and showed potential to upset the favored Michigan State Wolverines. Ultimately, the Wolverines's potent running game carried the game and the Beavers suffered a 34-7 loss. Oregon State has yet to return to the Rose Bowl.

Larry planned the return trip to Oregon to coincide with Shirley's drive north. They enjoyed another dinner together, this one in Stockton with two of Shirley's friends who were hobbyist vintners. Wine turned the evening romantic.

He returned to the hotel to see his boys had devoured their takeout dinner and entertained themselves with reruns of the naval drama, *Convoy*.

A few days after returning to Medford, Larry's neighbor Mary called.

"You ought see Ann again," she said.

"Ann?" He'd been focused on Shirley.

"Known her since the Camp-Fire Girls," Mary said, "I can tell when she likes someone."

Meanwhile, Ann was preparing to leave for work. Mary intercepted her in the driveway with the news that she had called Larry on her behalf.

"You didn't need to do that," Ann said.

"Boys need fathers," Mary said.

"I've been married—all I remember is the bad." The death of Ann's first husband was bad enough, but the betrayal by her second husband had devastated Ann.

At the time of meeting Larry, Ann had been single for

nine years. She had rarely dated during that time and instead found happiness in work, politics, and the philosophy of Ayn Rand. Ann was an oddity in the small town of Medford. Very few men knew what do make of someone like her, and she assumed Larry likewise would be confounded and move on.

Thus Larry's invitation to dinner was a surprise. Ann felt it was true, what Mary had said about boys needing fathers. She worried her boys, Chuck and Jerry, were at a disadvantage. Their primary male role model was Ann's brother Bob, who was starting a family of his own. Finding a father for her boys was something that Ann had nearly given up on. Her dips into the dating pool convinced her not all men were father material. She thought that Larry, a father of three boys, might prove the opposite.

Ann and Larry met for dinner and dancing at the Dardanelles restaurant in Gold Hill. Larry was familiar with the restaurant because its location halfway between Medford and Grants Pass facilitated meetings between engineers from the two cities. Dardanelles was a small settlement from the mid-eighteen hundreds that became famous when one of its hills became an active gold mine, leading to incorporation as Gold Hill in 1895.

Dinner was pleasant, and the dancing was memorable. Beatlemania was at its peak and the jukebox stocked many of their chart toppers, including *I Want to Hold Your Hand*, *She Loves You*, and *Love Me Do*.

Afterward, Larry dropped Ann off at her house then drove home. When he pulled into his driveway he fortunately caught a glimpse of his reflection in the rear-view mirror. His straw colored hair was disheveled and he had a bright red lipstick smear on his cheek. He smoothed back his hair and used his pocket-square to scrub away the lipstick. He didn't need a houseful of boys getting the wrong idea.

Larry remained a man of two minds, caught between the exciting appeal of Ann who challenged his view of women and Shirley who was familiar and safe. At the time, Larry had a busy schedule with three boys at home, a full time job with the California-Oregon Power Company (COPCO), part time contract work as an electrical engineer for architects, volunteering for the Medford Planning Commission, and his primary two service clubs, United Way and Kiwanis. The latter held a fundraiser called the Kiwanis Kapers. Larry gave Shirley tickets to the show.

Kiwanis Kapers was a scripted variety show. The major stage acts included full painted backdrops, props, and large ensemble casts. The highlights of the show included *The Dawn of Time*—Cave Men and Women in a comedy about primitive times—sequences from *Marc Antony and Cleopatra*, and a chorus of Magicians dressed as Devils. Larry was cast in the show as a mad scientist who would frequently electrocute himself on stage. Unknown to Larry, Ann was also part of the show, cast in a sketch about modern gender roles. Her costume was split down the middle with the right side that of a woman and the other that of a man.

After the show, in the backstage area where the performers mingled, Ann saw Larry. Even dressed as a mad scientist, he looked dashing with his clean-cut jaw and slicked back hair. During their first date, he had been very formal and polite. During the second date, while dancing he had been more flirty and romantic. Now, as she watched him from across the room he was jovial and lively as he re-enacted being electrocuted for anyone who talked to him. She couldn't help but smile at his glee. As she crossed the room to greet him, another woman approached and gave Larry a friendly hug and kiss on the cheek.

Ann paused. She had been warming to Larry and now surmised in an instant that she wasn't the only woman he had been courting. Ann remembered an offhand comment Larry had made about attending Parents without Partners. She had been to a similar group once decided groups like that led to meeting the wrong people for the wrong reasons. She hadn't expected the highly particular Larry to be one of those types.

Ann had a habit of comparing the men she met to her late husband, Chuck, who had eyes only for her. In a way, Ann romanticized Chuck the way the young do with their first serious love. Now, Ann watched Larry from across the room. It broke her heart to see his flirty body language as he talked to the unknown woman. Ann hurried to the dressing rooms.

Larry never saw Ann at the Kiwanis Kapers. He went on to visit Shirley several times before taking both of their families for an outing to Glendale, Oregon. It was a cozy getaway. Shirley marshaled the combined seven youths— four of hers and three of Larry's—with the natural grace of a mother. Watching his boys and Shirley's kids together reminded Larry of past times—with Marty.

2

Oregon Trail
Kansas 1941

At the age of fifteen, Larry brimmed with restlessness. He woke early and forced his feet into size-too-small shoes before helping his father load the car. The family was selling their small country house and moving to Oregon. Their 1934 Chevrolet Four Door became encumbered with suitcases, boxes, and what furniture it would hold. Even the chicken coops were lashed to the roof of the car. Larry and his father, Gene, finished packing under the sweltering late-day September heat.

"That's the last of it," Gene said.

When the film adaptation of *The Grapes of Wrath* had been released the previous year, Larry had been fortunate enough to see it in Dodge City. Their over-loaded car reminded him of a scene from the film. He squeezed into the backseat of the Chevy sedan with his siblings and watched the small Kansas house recede in the rear window.

It was a small plot of land where the family had grown food and kept chickens. It was where Larry had his first stirrings of entrepreneurialism—he used his .22 rifle to hunt rabbits for their pelts, and bought a set of rubber type so he could print penny newspapers. Life had been difficult, as Gene's sixth-grade education had made finding more than seasonal work a challenge. The move to Oregon would secure year-round employment for Gene at the Copeland Lumber Mill.

The drive west followed the approximate route of the Oregon Trail through Nebraska, Wyoming, Idaho, and finally along the Colombia River into Oregon where languid rains, the awe-inspiring Multnomah Falls, and the rugged, mountainous terrain was a shocking contrast to the dry, flat plains of Kansas.

Their destination, Portland, Oregon, started as an inland port along the Willamette River where ocean-going vessels could unload cargo destined for local settlements. Thousands of trees had been cleared for the city, their stumps painted white to make them visible against the mud created by seemingly constant rainfall. Because of all the white stumps, one of Portland's earliest nicknames was Stumptown. By the 1940s, Portland had become a thriving metropolis, the fourth most populated city on the West Coast behind Los Angeles, San Francisco, and its sister-city Seattle.

The Hortons rented a hundred-year-old house on SW Fourth near College and Hall. Larry helped his father unpack the car before setting out to explore his new surroundings. Just as he'd imagined, the city was full of opportunities—he promptly took a newspaper route. Hard work grew his subscriber base to over two hundred and won him a Thanksgiving turkey.

City life suited Larry just fine until just a few short months after they'd moved, H.V. Kaltenborn reported over the radio, "Japan has made war upon the United States without declaring it. Airplanes presumably from aircraft carriers have attacked the great Pearl Harbor base on Oahu."

World War II quickly changed Portland's nighttime skyline. A dimming zone had been enacted due to rumors of a Japanese submarine stationed at the mouth of the Columbia River. Portland and the surrounding cities were forced to stay dark, adding shutters and dimmers to any lights that could be seen from sea or the Columbia waterway, including car headlights. This made driving at night problematic for the recently licensed Larry. While his father's new job at a lumber mill brought in more income than the family was used to, wartime rations of chocolate, sugar, cheese, meats, and more kept their pantry as barren as it had been in Kansas.

As World War II escalated, Larry continued his studies. His mother, Retta, had always promoted education as the best way to provide for his future. Larry had taken her advice to heart. It began Larry's lifelong commitment to self-betterment.

The summer before Larry's senior year in high school, his double cousin, and all around best pal, Bill Horton approached him and said, "We should get jobs."

"I've got my paper route," Larry said.

"Real jobs. Not donut money," Bill said.

Larry felt the restlessness return to him: a real job, making his way in the world. "Fine. But no dishwasher type jobs," Larry said. He got enough of the dishes at home.

They were agreed and applied at a staffing agency.

Larry interviewed at one company that didn't hire him but liked him enough to recommend him to W.E. Finzer & Co. who took him on as a delivery boy and warehouseman. For deliveries, Larry rode a bicycle with an undersized front wheel and a large front basket for paper, ink, and address labels.

Marvin Finzer dazzled Larry. The businessman knew how to make money and always seemed to say the right thing. During meetings, Finzer would rapid-fire questions and statements, getting a quick summation of the week's business. Larry meekly fumbled his way through asking for time off to attend a church activity.

"If you're ever in a meeting and you got something to say, why speak up!" Finzer told him. "Don't mumble, just stand up and speak out." Even in rebuke, Finzer inspired Larry. To become more like the businessman, Larry sought to fix his public speaking deficit by joining the debate club.

One afternoon Bill called to tell Larry, "I'm going to war." The US Army had drafted Bill while he was still attending high school in 1943. He became a stretcher-bearer and saw heavy combat during the campaign leading up to the liberation of Rome. He went on to participate in Operation Dragoon where the Allies launched an amphibious attack on the German-occupied South of France. During the invasion, he captured twelve Germans in a pill-box. He was armed only with a stretcher at the time. After the war, Bill said, "There is a fine line between bravery and stupidity."

Larry, however, had been classified 4-F by the draft board—unfit for military service—due to his flat feet and heart murmur. Like many in the greatest generation, he felt a strong patriotic desire to do his duty for his nation, and Larry's growing habit of self-improvement convinced him he could become fit for service. He sought out help from Coach Keene.

"Get lots of sunshine," Keene said, "we'll get you in shape yet." Sunshine was Keene's codeword for exercise. He started Larry in a rigorous cross-training regimen including calisthenics, boxing, trampoline, and volleyball.

When he wasn't training, Larry spent his free time with the youth group at Clinton Kelly Methodist Church. One of their outings was a three-day conference in McMinnville. A nervous Larry climbed the steps of the church bus. His heart pounded as he sat next to a cute brunette from another youth group in town. Larry was hardly a ladies man. He had yet to be on an actual date, and rarely talked to girls outside of school.

The girl returned his furtive, flirty smiles. Larry had seen her before but had never gotten acquainted. This bus ride would remedy that if only Larry could find the guts to speak. He tried to imagine what Finzer would say in such a situation. Fortunately, she spoke first, "It looks like we're sharing a seat." She smiled sweetly.

Larry nearly blurted out, *Hey sugar, are you rationed*, but his shyness got in the way and all he managed to wrangle from his mouth was, "What a gas. I'm Lawrence Horton."

"Lawrence?" She scrunched up her face. "I'm Margaret Cowles, but everyone calls me Marty."

He had been going as Lawrence as long as he could remember, but something about this young woman eased his normally tight-laced demeanor. "You can call me Larry." He smiled. Marty and Larry. He liked the way that sounded. Apparently she did too and they soon began dating.

After Larry graduated from Franklin High School, he attended Willamette University on scholarship. Due to his failing the draft boards, he was one of the few civilian men on campus, a distinction that made him sought after by the eligible women. Fortunately Willamette was close enough to Portland that Larry could bring Marty down for weekends. She stayed at the Tri Delta sorority house and Larry was able to remain steady with his favorite girl.

During his time at Willamette, Larry worked on the school newspaper. They shared a print press with the Salem Statesman. It was late in the afternoon on April 12th, 1945 when chilling news came over the wire.

"We need to pull the type," Larry said.

They did. Their headline soon read "Roosevelt Dead." The longest serving President of the United States had died of a cerebral hemorrhage.

Larry called Marty that night. "We scooped the President's death," he said. The Statesman wouldn't be able to cover the story until the next morning's printing. That wasn't all the news he had for her. "All that training with Coach Keene paid off. I'm 1-A in the draft." He was nineteen years old and this was one of his first tastes of conquering adversity and it quickly turned bitter-sweet.

"There's going to take you! You're getting straight A's!" Marty's voice flooded with emotion.

"Other than German," he corrected, "just a B there."

"All the more reason not to go. You won't understand when they're trying to surrender," she said. Her voice cracked as she said it.

Larry laughed.

"This is serious," she said.

"I want to do my duty," Larry said. He felt certain he would be chosen by the draft. "What about the Navy?" The ROTC sailors on campus were doing their duty and getting an education in RADAR. "I can study for the Radio Technician exam."

He enlisted while Marty entered nurses training at the Good Samaritan Hospital in Portland. He was drafted after the end of the European theater of war and called up the last week in July. It would have been easier to remain 4-F and continue as a civilian, but the call to duty was too strong.

The Portland sky was uncharacteristically blue when Larry and Marty said their goodbyes on the ramp at Portland Union station. It wasn't how either of them wanted the relationship to end. Larry got down on one knee and presented Marty with a ring. "Will you marry me?"

"Yes." She wept. "Just come back to me Larry. I don't want to be a widow before I can be a wife." They kissed.

He remained strong and stoic for her as he boarded the train and waved out the window as they chuffed from the station. He was bound for Fort Lewis for his physical and serial number, then on to Seattle for induction to the Navy.

3

Hometown Girl
Medford 1941

Ann Butler made figure eights on the smooth ice at Ice Arena on Grape Street in Medford. At the top of each eight she switched edges with a twirl, spin, or other flourish.

Ruth skated by. "Isn't this much better than that miserable Icehouse Lake?" Ruth's father had just opened the facility two months ago, the first indoor rink in Southern Oregon, so his daughter could practice year round. Her goal was to join the "Hollywood Ice Revue" which featured the famous Norwegian figure skater and film star, Sonja Henie.

Ann, however, missed the old lake's charm. While electricity was becoming available in the Rogue Valley, allowing the adoption of modern refrigerators, Ann's mother wasn't ready to part with the reliable family icebox —essentially a shelved unit with a space for a large block of slowly melting ice. This gave Ann's father, Arnel, an excuse to take the family with him to Icehouse Lake to buy blocks of ice at the source. Skating at the lake made the trip worthwhile. While the old lake was magical, the indoor rink was convenient and allowed Ann and her brother Bob to join the Crater Skaters Club. Arnel was skilled on skates and helped them practice technical elements and routines.

While Ann hadn't begun jumps yet, she was getting comfortable with the occasional fancy turn. This time she did a double. The PA system squawked to life: "Breaking news on the War! The Japanese have bombed Pearl Harbor!"

Ann and her family returned home to gather around the radio for the latest news broadcasts. Besides keeping up with events, the family did what they could to help out the war effort locally. Ann's mother, Elsie, tended a Victory Garden while Arnel became an Air Raid Warden. His duties included being prepared to fight fires with his chemical fire extinguisher and to guide people to shelters in case of attack.

Five days after the attack on Pearl Harbor, Congress appropriated hundreds of acres of the local Agate Desert. It became a training facility named Camp White. Today, the remains of the camp have become the unincorporated White City, but at the time, it quickly became the second largest city in Oregon. This influx of capital and population became a catalyst for Medford's growth from a rural settlement to a regional hub of commerce.

Congress spent more than $27 Million on Camp White, which bolstered the local economy. Ann's first introduction to money, however, came from her brother Bob's burgeoning paper route. He often flaunted a new set of plastic Army Men, or slides for his View-Master, goading Ann to ask her parents for permission to start working. Only thirteen at the time, her parents agreed to let her work at her grandfather's jewelry store.

John Lawrence had moved from St. Paul, Minnesota to Medford, Oregon in 1908. Soon after John's arrival, he was able to buy the entire stock of the bankrupt Jeschke Jewelry Store for $500. He began business with a simple motto, "Don't worry about your competitor—worry about yourself." His dedication to always doing the right thing made business flourish. He sold watches, clocks, and jewelry, and was self-styled as, "J.F. Lawrence, the man who fixes watches that run." A fire in 1911 forced John to move his business into a joint location with a millinery—a place that designed and fabricated hats. After his wife, Julia died from carcinoma in her shoulder bone, John married Thora Smith. Together they rebranded "Lawrence the Jeweler" to Lawrence's Jewelers. John's oldest daughter, Elsie, married Arnel Butler, the descendent of one of John's earliest business rivals. Ann became the third generation to work at the store.

"If I'm going to be paying you, you're going to be working," were her grandmother Thora's first instructions.

At Lawrence's Jewelers, Ann delivered packages to the post office, kept the display cases free of finger-print smudges, dusted china and generally tried to stay out of Thora's way. Occasionally, however, Ann ran out of busywork and became the focus of Thora's scrutiny.

"You shouldn't wear your hair down," Thora said, "your forehead is already small. You want a boy to like you, don't you?"

Bangs were the fashion at the time, but Ann took Thora's advice and began styling her hair up, giving her a more cosmopolitan look than her peers. While the look did get Ann more attention, it also set her apart enough that boys didn't know what to make of her.

Ann continued to apply herself at the store, enough so that John noticed his granddaughter's strong work ethic and earnest attitude. He told her, "Thora are I are going out of town the next two days. I'm putting you in charge of the store."

Ann gulped. A thirteen-year old manager? Her nerves almost got the best of her, but she arrived first thing in the morning and opened the door. She wasn't going to let her grandparents down. A steady stream of soldiers from Camp White came to have their watches serviced and to buy jewelry for their gals. Ann even sold a diamond ring. The employees all congratulated Ann on a successful first day in charge.

"I'm just relieved everything went well," Ann said.

When she wasn't working at the store, Ann enjoyed the radio shows *The Shadow* and *McGee and Molly*. The former for its mystery, the latter for the comedy.

Her brother Bob often imparted wisdom to her like, "There's nothing new to invent," and, "The most important thing you can learn is a trade." Bob went on to learn the family business of watch repair.

Meanwhile, Ann's mixture of artistic sensibility from her father and educational pragmatism from her mother left her unsure what direction to take in life. She eventually enrolled in the University of Oregon's pre-nursing program where she joined the sorority Alpha Delta Pi. During a mixer co-hosted by one of the fraternities on campus, her sorority sisters introduced her to a young man named Chuck Wirkkula, whose parents had emigrated from Oulu, Finland.

Chuck was dashing and joyous. He had served in the

Navy during World War II, and was now halfway to graduating with a degree in Business. Beyond that he was caramel haired, blue eyed, and had a foreign charm even though he had been raised in America. It was love at first sight.

A whirlwind romance followed. She visited his family in Astoria, Oregon. His mother, who spoke with a Finnish accent, served the family dinner and ate later in the kitchen. Chuck's brother, Reino, had a claw-like hand that had been maimed from grabbing a rooftop power line as a child. Even with the injury, Reino and Chuck worked summers as fishermen on the Columbia River to earn money for school. Their father had passed away during Chuck's youth.

"How did he die?" Ann asked.

"He turned to stone," Chuck said.

"No, really?"

"Really."

It was a rare disease erroneously named the Stone Man Syndrome. Essentially, his muscles ossified into bone, locking his joints in place, working from his toes upward until it reached his heart.

"Tell me something more cheerful," Ann said.

"Anything you want!" His smile always glowed.

"Tell me of the Navy."

For a moment Chuck grew distant but it didn't take long for his easy smile to return. "Another time. The hospital ship was less fun than talking about your beauty."

They visited Ann's family in Medford where Chuck impressed her parents with his pleasant demeanor and industrious nature. Being the first of his family to graduate from college helped too.

When they returned to Eugene, he had surprising news for Ann. "I'll be moving to Portland for work."

Ann was devastated. "We'll never see each other." Neither of them had a car—Chuck hadn't learned to drive anyway. "Find work here!" Ann pleaded.

"All the opportunities are in Portland. And my family's there. It's home…you could come with me." His dashing grin accompanied a simple engagement ring. Ann's breath caught. She had just finished her Sophomore year. Her mother wished for her to graduate but as much as Ann liked college, she liked Chuck more.

"Yes," she said.

They were married in September at St. Mark's Episcopal Church by Father Bolster. It was one of the few dry months in the Pacific Northwest. They rode a ferry to Victoria, British Columbia for their honeymoon.

Over Tea, the newly minted Ann Wirkkula practiced her pronunciation. "Mrs. Charles Work-you-lah."

"Veer-kuu-luu," he corrected.

"Vir-kah-loo."

Chuck laughed. "No. No. More practice."

When they returned to Portland, they moved into an upstairs apartment. Chuck found work at Safeway.

It was late January when Ann realized she missed her period. While too early to see a doctor for confirmation, she was certain of the pregnancy. Still in the honeymoon stage, this child made Ann's love for Chuck burn brighter. She decided to tell him of the pregnancy on Valentine's Day.

Everything was to be perfect. She splurged for his favorite meal: fresh caught Columbia Salmon, a glass of wine, some aged cheese.

Her plans were interrupted two days before Valentine's Day when Chuck came home early from work. He was drowsy and having trouble focusing. Ann felt his head. He was burning up. They still didn't have a car—Portland's mass transit had been sufficient for them to navigate town —she called for an ambulance. Soon, Chuck became increasingly disoriented. The ambulance arrived and took him up the hill to the hospital that would later become OHSU. Chuck was unconscious on arrival and dead by the time Ann reached the hospital.

Ann ate salmon alone while listening to Ella Fitzgerald and Louis Armstrong, backdropped by the patter of ceaseless Portland winter rain.

Charles "Chuck" Ruben Wirkkula died on Feburary 12th, 1951. The final autopsy listed the cause of death as encephalitis as a complication of the poliovirus. Jonas Salk's inactivated polio vaccine wouldn't come into widespread use for another four years.

Chuck would be survived by a son who would never meet him.

4

End of the War
San Diego 1945

When Larry entered boot camp, he was one hundred and fifty-four pounds. The Navy set about changing that in a drastic way. Their first tactic was food. At home Larry had competition for food with his two brothers and a sister. At Willamette he had been a houseboy, getting occasional meals at the sorority house where he worked while otherwise eating like a typical starving college student. Now, however, he had the opportunity to devour endless portions of food. He loved it all. If there was one thing that boot camp liked soldiers to do more than eat, it was exercise. Calories from the mess hall turned into thirty pounds of bulking muscle.

Two weeks after Larry's arrival at boot camp, the first Atom bomb was dropped on Hiroshima. Three days later a more powerful bomb was dropped on Nagasaki. Just five days after that, Emperor Shôwa decreed to accept the terms of the Potsdam Declaration, offering surrender. World War II was over. The Navy began a gradual draw-down of its forces. During this time, Larry's training continued. When the company went to Camp Pendleton to learn to shoot M16s on the Marine Firing Range, Larry distinguished himself with top marks. He figured all the rabbit hunting he had done in Kansas made him a deadeye.

At the conclusion of boot camp, Larry was sent to Chicago by train for preliminary radio school at Manley High School. When he wasn't studying, he was able to take his first subway and elevated rail ride, attended his first professional football game, and visited the University of Chicago Museum of Science and Industry.

It wasn't all sight seeing, however. During one of practice builds, Larry built a simple electric motor. When he showed it to the proctor, he said, "It's a parallel circuit."

"Not the way you built it," the proctor said.

Larry was learning the basics of electricity: parallel versus series circuits. Series circuits worked where all devices were connected to one wire, like an old fashioned style of Christmas tree lights where one burnt out bulb would darken the entire strand. Lights arranged in parallel can burn out without affecting the rest of the lights.

The next stop in Larry's Navy education took him to Monterey California for electronic technician training. Returning to the West Coast gave Larry an idea when Christmas leave came around.

"I'd like to go to Portland," he told the company commander.

"No. It's too far."

"Where can I go in Oregon?"

"Klamath Falls." The Navy relied on train travel for its enlisted men and Klamath Falls was along the Southern Pacific Railroad.

Larry doubted Marty could make it to Klamath Falls, so he decided to hitchhike the rest of the way to Portland. It was worth risking trouble with the Navy for a chance to kiss his fiancé.

Marty rented a basement apartment in the house next-door to Larry's parents. After he stowed his bag with them, he paid her a visit.

"Are they still treating you well?" she asked.

"You should see the place they have us. Hotel Del Monte." He held up his hands in an attempt to capture the grandeur of the former luxury resort hotel that had been leased to the Navy as a training facility. "There's a horse track, golf course, and of course access to the beach. Can you believe I went swimming in January? There's even a Roman plunge pool."

"There better not be girls in those new swim suits on the beach!" Marty gave him a glare. Fabric shortages during the war had led to the government requiring a 10% reduction in fabric for women's swimwear. Bared midriffs got wider, and skirts and other flourishes were removed. Jaques Heim, a French designer continued this trend and created the modern bikini.

"Just a bunch of sailors." Larry laughed. "How's nursing school?"

Marty was enrolled in the Nursing Program at the Good Samaritan Hospital. "Not well," she said, "I get a headache every time I start on Math."

"I'll tutor you." Larry had excelled at mathematics in high school.

"How about the cinema, instead?" Marty smiled. "*Spellbound* is playing." It was Alfred Hitchcock's 37th film as Director and starred Ingrid Bergman and Gregory Peck who had a brief affair on set.

Upon completing training at Del Monte, Larry's rank was increased to Electronic Technician Mate 3rd Class. Radio and sonar school was conducted on Treasure Island in the San Francisco Bay. In addition to hands-on training with Navy equipment, Larry pulled Shore Patrol and Water Taxi duty, the former to keep sailors from being too rowdy on leave and the latter to make sure they returned to base safely.

During weekend leave, Larry and a friend from the base hitchhiked to Yosemite. They climbed to the top of the falls and enjoyed the breathtaking valley views. Instead of returning along the trail they took in, they took an alternate route which was significantly longer than they had expected. By the time they got back to the parking lot, the park had closed. They found a payphone and called into base in attempt to avoid an Away Over Leave judgement.

"We're stuck in Yosemite," Larry said.

"What do you mean stuck?"

"We hitchhiked in. We took too long getting off the mountain. Everyone's gone," Larry said.

The officer of the watch offered no solace.

Larry and his friend camped overnight. In the morning, visitors returned to the park and Larry and his friend were able to hitchhike back to base. When they showed up at the gate, they were taken to the brig for being Away Over Leave. They appeared before Captain's Mast where they had all leave privileges revoked.

Larry used this time to dedicate himself to studying and soon passed the test to become Electronic Technician

Mate 2nd Class. The Navy discharged him in July of 1946, before he was able to complete radio training. He received GI benefits so he was able to apply to Oregon State College (renamed to Oregon State University in 1961) and by changing his major to Electrical Engineering he was able to keep some of the experience and training from the Navy.

5

Think and Grow Rich
Portland 1946

Larry enjoyed returning home and spending the summer with Marty. By then she had dropped out of nursing school and worked at Montgomery Ward. Larry took on summer employment and they saw each other evenings. When he left for college in the fall, he felt the same heartbreak at having to leave his gal that he had felt when going into the Navy. Corresponding by mail helped somewhat but when he attended his sister's wedding in early November, Larry decided he couldn't put off marriage any longer. He sent Marty a telegram that read: "Wedding Bells." She too was eager to be married.

Both of their families were poor. Marty's father was a clerk at a dry goods store, and Larry's father was delivering lumber for Copeland Yards. They didn't have the money for a lavish wedding. The ceremony was held at the Sellwood Methodist church over Thanksgiving break in 1946 with the ministers from each of their respective churches sharing the duties of officiating. Larry was twenty years old and Marty was nineteen years old. They honeymooned near Mount Hood in a snowed-in cabin.

They moved into married housing on campus. The GI bill gave a living stipend of $120 a month and covered tuition and books. To supplement room and board, Larry worked at the library, campus maintenance, and as a Physics lab assistant.

During the following summer break, Larry and Marty became fire spotters for the Forest Service. Their lookout was on a flattened part of a mountain south of Mt Rainier. It was a small building with glass on all sides, a table with an elevation map of the surrounding area, a phone, a bed, and not much else. Their training instructor left them with one piece of advice: "If there's lightning, get on the bed—it's an insulator." The nearest ranger station was a seven-mile hike. Larry's marksmanship hadn't diminished since the Navy and he shot a grouse that Marty cooked for dinner. For the most part, they were alone on what felt to Larry as a second honeymoon.

"Smoke," Marty said in the morning. It was an inky black plume to the West in the Valley. They checked the map and got their best guess at coordinates before calling it in. A few hours later the ranger called them back. Just a farmer burning illegally.

When the lightning came, they did as the forest ranger had suggested, and took shelter on the bed. The storms were fantastic from atop the mountain. Larry held Marty close and they let nature's light show backdrop their romantic mountaintop getaway. Their first son, Craig was born nine months later.

Larry began transitioning from school to professional employment during his senior year by splitting time between education and work at the Mountain States

Power Company in Albany. His grades began to slip, at the lowest he earned a 2.0 GPA until he turned things around by adding a minor that Larry took to with natural ease: Business in Electrical Engineering. The courses on corporate finance, business law, and accounting seemed instinctive to Larry. He was the first in his family to graduate college. A few months later, Larry's family grew by one with the birth of Lawrence Stanley Horton Jr., who they called Stan.

The most influential book Larry read after graduation was Napoleon Hill's *Think and Grow Rich*. The book had a profound effect on the already industrious Larry. Growing up in poverty had instilled a drive for wealth, and the book inspired a faith that he could succeed for his family. As he explained it to Marty, "It's all right here in the book. Plan your work, and work your plan."

"By conquering fear of poverty and embracing ambition, I can demand however many riches I need to be satisfied."

Marty rubbed her pregnant belly. She had inherited a little money from her parents to pay the hospital bill when Craig had been born, however, paying for Stan out of pocket had strained their budget, and this third baby would strain it further. "A little extra money wouldn't be bad," she said.

Larry quickly found another place, in the middle of the book. "It even tells me how to become a leader. All I have to do is be an astute follower of someone successful." Specialized knowledge like Electrical Engineering made him valuable to others who were also looking to succeed.

"Do you have someone in mind?" she asked.

"Jack Draper," he said.

"Will he want to?"

"He gave me this book." Larry grinned. And the book had planted the seeds of Larry's future success.

Jack and his wife Barbara Draper attended the same Methodist church as the young Horton family. In addition to his work with the power company, Larry took on part time work drafting and consulting for Jack Draper. They moved to "Draperville," a country living community outside of Albany.

Jack Draper and his wife were both in the middle of building political campaigns. Jack was running for US Congress.

"Larry, I need people in my organization that can fly," Draper told him, "If you want to learn, you can use my plane. I'll even pay for lessons."

The idea sounded marvelous to Larry. Draper's plane was an Ercoupe 415-C. It was considered the safest monoplane that aerospace engineers could design at the time. It featured fixed tricycle landing gears, seating for two, a wooden propeller and no rudder paddles or radio. Its 65 horsepower engine gave it a cruising speed of 95 miles per hour. Seven hours of training later, Larry flew the plane to Lebanon for his final exam.

After completing the exam, the proctor asked, "Did someone drop you off?"

"No."

"How'd you get here then?" the proctor asked.

"I flew."

"You are supposed to take this exam before you solo." The proctor knit his brows. "Well. You passed so I guess it's all right."

Larry, grinning ear to ear, flew back to Albany. It

seemed nothing could stop him. He even convinced the Board of Engineering to let him to take his Registered Engineer's Exam early. They required a minimum of two years on the job under 'Responsible Charge,' but Larry persuaded them that the year he had spent working part time at the power company while still enrolled at college should count. They let him take the test early. He passed.

As election season neared, Jack Draper called Larry for help. "If you could just get your vacation for two weeks and work for me during that time, I'll give you one thousand dollars."

Larry quickly agreed. He was making around $300 a month at the Power Company, and the extra money would come in handy with household expenses. At the end of the first week, Larry received $250. At the end of the second, Draper told him, "I just don't have the money. Will you take my airplane instead?"

The airplane had a value of $500. While the airplane didn't help with the household expenses, Larry hoped using it for getaways would aid Marty with her headaches. He took her on day trips as far as Coos Bay and to closer destinations like a Camp Magruder where he got the plane stuck in soft sand during a beach landing.

The next day he rolled the plane to the hard sand to fly it home. It was unstable in the air, and on landing, he discovered the beach landing had worn off part of the wooden propeller. He had it replaced with a steel propeller. When Marty told him the getaways weren't helping with her headaches, Larry decided to trade the plane in to a local flying club in exchange for $500 worth of credit towards future flying time. It was easier than storing and maintaining the aircraft himself.

The birth of Steven in 1951 brought another bundle of joy into the house, but it also brought pain. Marty's headaches worsened, sometimes making it difficult for her to do much more than keep the kids fed and the diapers washed.

"I'm having trouble keeping up with them," Marty admitted.

"Three feels like a good amount of kids," he said.

"Three is plenty." Marty managed to smile through the pain of her headache.

Birth control pills were still a decade away from widespread use and the easiest way to avoid another pregnancy was a vasectomy.

Other attempts to improve Marty's health included family camping trips to the Cascades where they could get plenty of fresh air and vigorous exercise, activities with the Methodist Church, and even buying a television for $50. From Albany, however, they could only get one station and that one was mostly snow.

Unable to find a solution for Marty's headaches, Larry refocused his vitality towards business success. Realizing he needed, as Napoleon Hill called it, a larger "Master Mind Alliance," he joined the Corvallis Engineers Club. Through training seminars he learned about symmetrical components, transformers, capacitors, distribution lines and substations. His growing education didn't stop there. Soon the Mountain States Power Company merged into Pacific Power and Light. As part of this new company, Larry studied atomic energy at the Hanford Nuclear Power Plant. He spent weeks in Richland, Washington and weekends in Albany with his family.

The heavy commute strained Larry. The lengthy

absences seemed to exacerbate Marty's headaches. They needed a change. Larry leveraged his business minor to take a position in Pacific Power's Engineering Planning Office, in Portland. The move took their family to the Laurelhurst area of Portland.

They enjoyed spending their weekend afternoons in the park. Wide lawns, easy walk-paths, and a clear lake gave the boys places to play and the parents places to relax.

"How is it being back in Portland?" Larry asked.

"It's nice having my parents and yours nearby. I can usually find someone to help when my headaches come," Marty said. "How's the new job?" Marty asked.

"I'm bored to death," Larry said.

"Why don't you take a correspondence course, or something?"

It seemed a good idea to Larry. While signing up for a speed reading class, the recruiter asked him, "What do you hope to get out of speed reading?"

"It seems useful," Larry said. There was a lot of tedious reading in the planning department.

"I'll tell you what's useful, the Dale Carnegie class."

"What's that?" Larry asked.

"It teaches success." The recruiter grinned.

Larry hadn't shaken the seed of ambition planted from *Think and Grow Rich* and he liked the idea of taking a class on success. He signed up for "How to Win Friends and Influence People" and "How to Stop Worrying and Start Living." While the class gave away weekly awards for achievement, the only award Larry took home was most improved. His public speaking deficit was larger than his initial assumption, but the most improved gave him confidence he could remedy this shortcoming by joining

Broadway Toastmasters.

On September 27th 1955 at 3:05 in the afternoon the Civil Defense Authority rang sirens signaling the start of a practice evacuation of the Portland metropolitan area. The entire city of Portland shut down. Larry hurried back to Laurelhurst where he loaded the family into their car and fought traffic on his way out to Gresham. By 3:59PM nearly thirty-thousand vehicles and one hundred thousand people had evacuated downtown.

"Oh man! A Corvette Sting Ray" Craig exclaimed from the back seat. A couple years ago he had learned almost every type of car in production, and now at the age of seven, he excitedly identified the exotic ones. "Why are they shutting everything down?" Craig asked.

"In case there's another war," Larry said. He didn't want to tell his son about the destructive power of nuclear bombs. During his time in the Navy he had learned enough about them to know he wanted nothing to do with them.

Larry began a search for new opportunities. The most interesting one was in Medford, Oregon. It had a few advantages that appealed to Larry. First it would get him away from the metropolitan area. Next, it would allow him to best leverage what he had learned from the Carnegie Course and Toastmasters as a bigger fish in a smaller pond, and finally, he could get away from the rain. He hoped the dry climate would finally cure Marty of her headaches.

6

New Beginnings
Medford 1951

Ann watched Chuck's casket get lowered into the sodden ground on the south Hill of Veteran's Cemetery. As typical with Portland rain, it had been a light sprinkle for most of the week. For a moment it let up and Ann's breath hinted ghostly white before dissipating on the brisk air.

Her parents had arrived the previous night and stayed with Ann through the ceremony. She said her goodbyes to Chuck's mother, sister, and brother.

Ann barely remembered the five-hour drive south to her parents's home. Her bed was the same as when she had left it two and a half years ago. She sobbed more than slept that first night.

Across from her bed, on the shelf where her dolls had sat, were several dozen agates. Her father, Arnel, was a rock hound and had been actively collecting them from the former site of Camp White. The Army Corps of Engineers base had closed shortly after the end of World War II. The area where the base had been was fertile with agates—known commonly as thunder eggs. The blues, purples, pinks and salty whites of the stones glinted by morning sun.

Ann remained under the covers until she heard activity in the house. She got out of bed, still dressed in black from the funeral.

Downstairs, her mother, Elsie, made coffee.

"Did you sleep well?" Elsie asked.

Ann shrugged before sitting at the breakfast table and staring out the window. At length, she asked, "Where did my dolls go?"

"You'll have to ask your father," Elsie said.

Arnel entered from the living room with the daily newspaper tucked under his arm. "Did you sleep well?" he asked Ann.

Ann repeated her shrug.

Elsie had finished coffee and poured three mugs. Ann and her parents sat around the table. Arnel flipped the paper open.

"Any section you can part with?" Elsie asked.

"Sports, I suppose." Arnel handed a section across to his wife.

Ann fidgeted. She thought of her F&B doll. It seemed strange to bury a husband and return home to think of a doll. But the doll had been a favorite of hers and the familiarity of it gave her a hopeful reminder of a time before her heart felt heavy with grief. "Dad, where did you put my doll?"

"Doll?" Arnel flipped the paper up in front of his face.

"From my shelf. She had a seersucker dress. A black velvet cape—pink satin on the inside to match the dress."

"Oh." His voice pitched up.

"Do you know where it is?"

"My boss's wife collects dolls. I gave it to her. I thought
__"

"You'd do something for yourself." Ann said it more
bitterly than she intended and instantly felt a queer mix of
regret and sorrow.

"You had left home."

"For college."

"And…" her dad paused awkwardly "…for Portland."

"That was in September!" The marriage only had four
perfect months before complications of polio took Chuck's
life. Ann looked to her mother for help.

Elsie shared a gentle smile. "Just be glad your father is
home now."

Half a decade ago, Arnel had lost his job at the Jackson
County Savings & Loan. His attempts to sell real estate
locally hadn't worked out, forcing him to take a job at
Klamath Falls Savings & Loan, and later one in Bend with
a pumice excavation company. He had commuted during
the week and spent weekends with the family. Elsie taught
Math at Medford High and kept the kids in school as
opposed to relocating with Arnel's job changes.
Fortunately, Arnel's latest job brought him back to
Medford at the Jackson County Title Company where he
used enlargers and worked in the darkroom.

"I like what Len Casanova is doing with the Oregon
Ducks," Elsie said, changing the subject. "Give him a
couple years and I think they'll have a winning record
again. Speaking of the University of Oregon…do you
plan to return to school in the fall?"

"I can't," Ann said.

"Give it a few months and—"

"I'll be having a baby when the fall term starts." It was

the first time Ann admitted it out loud and she felt a mix of excitement and anxiety at the reveal.

"Oh, Ann, that's wonderful news considering everything that's happened!" Elsie's smile radiated joy.

Arnel folded his paper double. "Stay with us as long as you need."

"I couldn't impose…" Ann wasn't sure what else she would do.

"It'll be nice to have a baby in the house again," Elsie said.

It was a difficult time for Ann. Pregnancy hormones exacerbated her grief over Chuck's death. She gave birth to a son in the fall, naming him Charles Robert Wirkkula for his late father. The pink faced, screaming baby became the most important thing in Ann's life. She cared for the baby and did the cooking, cleaning, and other chores to maintain her parents's household.

When baby Chuck was old enough to stay with a sitter, Elsie sat down with Ann at the breakfast table.

"Thora isn't doing well," Elsie said. "She has the early signs of dementia and has been having trouble running the family jewelry store. Business is in decline. I have enough inheritance to buy Thora out. You can run the store with your brother." Bob had completed a course from Bradley University's School of Watchmaking and would be able to continue the traditions started by John Lawrence. There was a catch, however.

"Bob's at War," Ann said.

"Doing the weather on Johnston Island. He'll be home safe, I can feel it," Elsie said.

It had been a little more than four years since Ann had last worked at Lawrence's Jewelers. While Ann had been away, John Lawrence had died. Without a will, half of the store had passed to his wife, Thora, with the remaining quarters to his daughters, Ruth and Elsie. Thora had relocated the store to a smaller location at 130 E. Main Street. It was a narrow store, with display cases on one side and tables for china and gifts on the other side.

When Camp White had closed eight years prior, nearly thirty-thousand people had left the region, many of them were the young soldiers buying rings for their best gals, which had been the core of the jewelry store's business. With John's death, the store also lost watch repair which had been its last reliable source of income.

Elsie mentored Ann in the jewelry business. She started with the basics of sales, keeping the store clean, and eventually moved on to buying merchandise for the store. "John's death was hard on Thora," Elsie said. "She didn't take care of the store well after that. But there was something she understood, and that's the power of a strong brand. It's easier to sell something that people recognize."

"Is that why they changed it from Lawrence the Jeweler to Lawrence's Jewelers?" Ann asked.

"Not entirely. That was more complicated. But it allowed the store to continue after his death," Elsie said.

Ann thought about that a moment, then switched the subject. "Don't you get tired? Working here *and* teaching?"

"It's better to wear out than to rust out." Elsie's gentle smile beamed.

For the first Christmas at the store, Ann bought several dozen rolls of wrapping paper adorned with red and green ornaments and snowflakes. It was attractive and classy. After staring at the same pattern for dozens of rolls,

Ann said, "I'm getting sick of looking at this."

"We could get a few different styles next Christmas," Elsie said.

Ann shook her head. "It's like what you were telling me about making the store a brand. Everything should look the same, so people know it's a gift from Lawrence's. If we make our gifts special, it makes the store special...it helps the brand."

They agreed to keep the multi-colored handcrafted bows while changing the paper to elegant silver. Arnel supplied the finishing touch: a pinecone tied to the bow.

At the end of the Korean War, Bob returned home. Ann was glad to have him working with her at Lawrence's Jewelers. It gave her a chance to catch up with the brother she hadn't seen since graduating High School.

"How was it being in the war?" Ann asked.

"I was just doing the weather. It was kind of dull."

"At least you were on an island. The beaches must have been nice."

"It was all beach," he said. The island was a little bigger than a football field. The air force flew seaplanes in and out of the island. The only excitement Bob had was a couple of storms that forced the base to evacuate.

Bob's skills with watch repair added reliable income to the store. Much like his grandfather, he took care in his work. His education from watch making school had been robust enough that he could assemble watches from parts. In addition to watch repair, he brought elegant hand-engraving to the store. He could do free hand letters, background stippling, repeated patterns and the like.

"You make it an art," Ann told him.

* * *

Being a single working mom in the 1950s, Ann divided her time between Chuck and the store. When Wilbur came along, his dapper charm and willingness to court a single mother in a time when eligible women vastly outnumbered eligible men convinced her there was a chance that she could once again find the level of romance—if not love—that she had enjoyed with Chuck's father. When Wilber proposed marriage, Ann was overjoyed at the thought she could gain freedom from her parent's now overcrowded home and provide the toddling Chuck with a father figure.

They were married in 1954 and moved to Pendleton, Oregon where Wilbur worked. Ann used the Military Insurance money from Chuck Sr.'s death to buy a mobile home.

At first, Ann thought she might finally become a stay at home mom. Shortly after the birth of her second child, Jerry, she discovered that Wilbur was a homosexual. He hadn't married Ann for love like she first had thought, but instead to hide his sexual identity during a time when President Eisenhower signed an executive order which would among other effects establish 'sexual perversion' as ground for dismissal of federal employees. This was on the heels of Under Secretary of State John Peurifoy's comments about a 'homosexual underground' leading to the 'Lavender scare' that ran concurrent to the 'Red scare' of communism. While Ann didn't fault Wilbur for his sexual identity, she felt devastated that his intent towards her had not been genuine. She left him.

A resolve grew in Ann. She had already proven to herself that she could raise enough money to support her family, giving her the confidence to know that she wouldn't marry again for providence, but instead would only marry for companionship.

She returned to Medford. After filing for divorce, she sold the mobile home, making enough money for a down-payment on a house at the corner of Barneburg and Highland. Moving into a house of her own was a relief. Chuck could run wild without threatening to shatter all of Elsie's breakables or tear any of Arnel's prints. And Jerry wouldn't wake an entire household when he cried for a midnight feeding. Beyond the boys, Ann had always wanted a cat, and now that she was away from her father's German Shepherd, she finally could. She didn't just get one, she got two.

One afternoon, Chuck came running into the house. "Momma! Momma! The cat got run over!"

She followed her three year old outside. The cat limped across the street. Ann scooped up the cat and took it inside where she nursed it back to health. "I can tell we're going to be good friends," Ann told the cat. It agreed with a purr.

With two children to provide for, Ann needed to return to work. She made an arrangement with Mrs. Devanny, an employee at the jewelry store, which allowed Ann to watch both her kids and Mrs. Devanny's grandkids in the morning, and then they would switch in the afternoon. It was part-time employment, but it was employment.

In a way, the store became Ann's husband. She dressed nicely for the store, sophisticated in high heels, cosmetics and the works. She always wore earrings a necklace and the occasional ring because she was selling jewelry. She bought what she wore; she wouldn't wear something just to show it off—all of the jewelry for sale had to be new.

Just as a wife was expected to keep a husband fed and clothed, Ann bought for the store and arranged its decorations. While there were many other jewelry stores in the valley, Ann remembered her grandfather's advice, "Don't worry about the competition, worry about yourself."

There was plenty to worry about. She and Elsie had made a good start years ago, and Bob's repair skills had brought more business, but winning enough customers over to support two families hadn't been easy. Elsie was an efficient manager with excellent people skills and a head for doing books while Bob's practical skills were in constant demand. To further boost the store's visibility in the Rogue Valley, Ann began appearing in television advertisements on the locally produced weekly Joan Heisel Hornecher program. Because of Ann's appearances on the program, people began to recognize her around town.

"We need to grow the business," Ann told Elsie and Bob as they closed the store for the night.

"We already have the best watch repair in town," Bob said.

"The best still has competition," Ann said. "Let's do something nobody else in town is doing." Ann knew something drastic had to happen for the store to really become successful.

"What do you suggest?" Elsie asked.

"Marshall Fields has a bridal registry," Ann said.

"You can buy a bride?" Bob asked with a joking laugh.

Ann didn't dignify that with a response but instead explained, "Engaged couples come in and pick out china, silver, stemware, whatever they want. They write on their invitations that they're registered at Lawrence's. The guests don't have to remember the patterns or the manufacturers, just the name of the Bride or Groom."

The bridal registry became a business boon for Lawrence's Jewelers. The initial profits were good. Soon other stores attempted to duplicate their success. Bridal registries increased in popularity—one store in Ashland only did bridal registries. Even with growing competition, Elsie had continued John's Lawrence's tradition of always doing the right thing in customer service. That tradition, coupled with Ann's vision for the most upscale store in the region—one that could compete with Tiffany's or Zell Brothers of Portland—created a store that won customers for life.

Ann and her boys celebrated Thanksgiving with her parents and Bob. Turkey with cranberry sauce and stuffing, mashed potatoes, and because Arnel wanted to demonstrate just how ahead of his time he was, with a TV dinner—oven quick and tastes like home cooked.

Earlier in the year, McDonald's began opening franchises and the first Burger King opened. Cheap fast food was on its way to the American home. It's convenience would let Ann spend a little more time at the jewelry store while still giving her boys a warm dinner. At the time, however, she enjoyed her mother's legendary Thanksgiving feast. Roasted turkey stuffed with bread cubes, sage and gravy, accompanied by fresh crab, tomato aspic, oven fresh rolls, green beans and peas, sweet potatoes baked with marshmallows, and a rotating desert of mincemeat pie, pumpkin pie, or lemon meringue pie. And of course, there was always a dish of black olives.

At the end of the meal she helped herself to a candy from the dish Elsie kept in the dining room and joined the rest of the family in the sitting room. Elaborate carpets were spaced around the cold hardwood floor.

"Business is really picking up, we might need a bigger store," Bob said.

"I have an idea for a storefront. Black marble. Rounded windows." Arnel glowed when he talked design and art. "It would need something really amazing for the lettering. Something that would pop."

"Neon," Ann said.

"That would do it." Everyone nodded along with Arnel in agreement.

Ann pulled her mother aside. "I'm so grateful for everything you've done for me and the boys."

"I'm a grandmother. I'm supposed to spoil them. All I gave you was a shoulder to lean on when you needed it. You did all the rest." Elsie's smile was, as always, gracious.

7

Work and Faith
Medford 1955

Larry's new position with the California-Oregon Power Company (COPCO) placed him in charge of four men. He was responsible for special engineering projects, including the stabilization of a high-voltage line to Crescent City. Engineering consumed his time. When he wasn't working, he was writing papers, one of which was published in Electrical West.

While the hard work kept restlessness away, he felt a need to strive to do better. Fortunately, he didn't have to wait long for an opportunity. The Dale Carnegie class came to Medford. Since he had taken the course in Portland, he was able to volunteer as a graduate assistant. The course reinvigorated his desire for self-improvement and led Larry to join several social groups, some that he had attended while in Portland such as Toastmasters and the Independent Order of Odd Fellows (IOOF), and others that were new to him and his family such as the Elks Club for lunch and billiards and YMCA so he could have outings with his boys. With a full social calendar, he practiced Carnegie's art of being instantly like-able by becoming interested in others, smiling, remembering names, encouraging others to talk about themselves—his go-to move was to ask what they did for work—and to talk in terms of other people's interests.

One of the people he met was Architect Wayne Struble. "We're building a new junior high school in Ashland and we need an Electrical Engineer. Is that something you can do?" Struble asked.

Training from the Carnegie course was well ingrained in Larry and he didn't hesitate to point out his own shortcomings for the project. "Most of my experience is with primary energy delivery: voltage, capacitors, load systems. I avoided all the questions on the engineering exam that had to do with wiring and lighting."

"I'm sure you can do it," Wayne said. Another thing that Larry had learned from the Carnegie course was to let the other person do the talking and be sympathetic with their desires, which led to Wayne saying, "The power company has a monopoly on the certified Electrical Engineers in town. I understand you've done freelance work before. It would be a real boon to us if you could again."

"I'll get some books and study up," Larry offered.

"That would be great. I can get you early architectural drawings of the school tomorrow."

Larry convinced the power company that letting him learn and practice electrical codes would be a boon. As a mutual benefit he agreed to teach the codes to apprentices at the power company.

However, the task of designing electrical plans for a school quickly revealed itself to be a full time job. With his COPCO responsibilities consuming his days, Larry was forced to work nights to complete drawings and type out specifications. Fourteen-hour workdays became normal, with Larry habitually starting his day job at 8AM and ending his night job at 2AM.

Once word got out about the quality job he did on the school, more projects were arranged, one of the more famous being the Outdoor Theater for Shakespeare in Ashland and the Rogue Valley Country Club. The latter paid him in golf membership and dining—his frequent visits to the golf course slowly lowered his handicap to 17.

Everything seemed to be going Larry's way until his supervisor at the power company pulled him aside to say, "We like what you're doing here. You were short listed for a local management position in an outlying district. But..." The supervisor took an uncomfortably long pause. "This work you're doing on the side has been interfering too much. You need to stop. Pacific Power and Light is looking to takeover COPCO. They're not going to want you doing double duty."

Larry, emboldened by his success as a contractor, resigned. He sought more work through his social contacts. Harold Soballe convinced him that they should go into business for themselves as Mechanical Electrical Associates. Because of Medford's proximity to California, many of the jobs they got were in the Golden State, necessitating that Larry be licensed there. Larry met California's proctor in person. The test went something like this:

"How do you calculate voltage drop? How many foot candles of lighting in this room? How do you calculate fault current?"

Larry answered the questions with the quickness of

someone working these problems on a daily basis.

"You pass," the proctor said.

In the midst of these professional successes, Larry's youngest, Steve came down with a bad case of strep throat that turned into rheumatic fever. He was frequently complaining of chest pain. A trip to the family physician, Dr. Byers, ended with a chilling prognosis: "Steve's infection has taken a nasty turn. His rheumatic fever is escalating to rheumatic heart disease. Essentially, his immune system is mistaking his heart for foreign tissue and attacking it. It's a rare complication, but its almost always fatal."

"There's nothing we can do?" Larry asked.

"Bed rest and antibiotics." It was all Dr. Byers could proscribe.

They had a hospital-grade bed installed in the living room.

"This is why God had me take that nurses training in Portland," Marty told Larry, "So that I could care for my son."

Hospice care caused Steve to miss most of a year of school as Marty only let him out of the house for Sunday service. The family had helped establish St. Luke's Methodist Church on the East side of Medford where Marty sang with the choir.

"Mom, your solo was swell. You sounded like an angel up there," Steve told her.

Six months later, Steve was on the mend, although, not without lasting damage. The chronic inflammation twisted his heart and caused his left subclavian artery to re-route over his shoulder. It was a complication that would forever limit his athletic capacity.

Most importantly, he survived. As Marty explained it: "A gift from God."

Larry taught boys Sunday School. Even here, Larry utilized techniques he had learned from the Carnegie class. The first was to get people saying 'yes' early. To the class, he said, "Would you like to impress your parents?"

Of course the dozen boys answered yes.

"And would you like to learn more about the bible?" He asked.

The first yes continued through the second yes.

He knew that to hook the kids, he had to convince them that what he wanted to do was their idea. "What's something that every book in the Bible has?"

"Words!" One boy shouted.

"Well, yes."

"Verses!" Another boy called out.

"Those are both good observations." But they weren't what Larry wanted to talk about. The boys needed a gentle nudge. "What about at the beginning of each book?" Larry asked.

"Titles!" A third boy said. Exactly what Larry wanted them to think about.

"Do you think anyone could learn all of the titles in the Bible?" Larry asked. This was another of Carnegie's techniques: making a challenge.

"I could!" One boy said.

"I'd learn them better!" Another boy said.

Larry knew he had them now. "What if I told you I had a secret technique that would make it easy to learn the titles. Would you want to hear it?" Of course the kids said yes. "The first Book of the Old Testament is Genesis. To remember that name, I want you all to visualize the Earth looking like a rock before it had trees or water or air."

"What does visualize mean?" One boy asked.

"To make a picture in your mind," Larry said. He knew from experience that visual images were much easier to recall than words alone.

Larry continued to spend weekends with his family, and work days with an industrious dedication to working as often and hard as possible. His relentlessness earned enough money that they could buy a larger house. The lot Larry chose was the last lot in town with a view in two directions at 509 N Barneburg.

Beyond that, his dedication to Toastmasters led to a position on Medford's Planning Commission and to the opportunity to purchase a cabin on Anderson Butte Ridge. The 'A' frame cabin was without electricity, water, or a septic system. But it came with ten acres of land and was a good upgrade from the old, Army-style green canvas tent the family had been using for camping. To reach the cabin in the winter, Larry bought an old four wheel-drive Jeep. He only got it stuck in a snowdrift once.

Getaways to the cabin also failed to ease Marty's headaches. Out of desperation she went to a psychiatrist with hopes that it was somehow related to anxiety or stress. The psychiatrist had taken several pictures of her head and concluded, "You're not symmetrical. One side of your forehead is bigger than the other."

Computational Tomography, commonly known now as CT scans, was an emerging technology at the time and would not find widespread use for several years. The common technology at the time, Linear Tomography could only capture simple images at varied depths inside the brain.

Dr. Mario Campagna, a top Neurosurgeon, resided in the Rogue Valley. He sat down with Larry and Marty.

"The brain scan confirms the presence of a tumor over the right eye in the forehead," he told them, "X-ray doesn't give us a clear picture of the spread. We can operate. There's a fifty-fifty chance we can remove the tumor…and a chance the surgery could be fatal."

"And if you don't operate?" Marty asked.

Dr. Campagna focused his attention on Marty, "It's rare for a tumor to stop growing. My prognosis is that the headaches will continue until more significant brain damage occurs."

The next months were tense. Larry, for the first time in his adult life, was unable to make a decision. Partly because it was Marty's decision to make, and partly because her life was at stake.

"I think we should do the surgery," Marty said.

"He said it could kill you," Larry said.

"He's one of the best in the country! I studied enough nursing to know the medical industry—it's the best chance I have!" She spoke with fire and passion.

"I can't lose you," Larry said.

"What else do I do? Wait for the tumor to grow and make me blind? Rob me of my speech? Make it so I can't even recognize our children?" Her eyes verged on tears.

"We don't know what the complications could be!" Larry's usual composure vanished. He became primal man, nothing but instinct and need. His need was Marty. His instinct was to protect her. But his mind could not conceive how to protect her other than to concede, "If you're decided. You have my support."

The last time Larry and the boys saw her before her surgery, her head had been shaved. Dotted lines covered her skin, marking where incisions would be made to open her skull. She pulled on a simple cap to hide from the boys's stares.

"Don't worry mom, we'll pray every minute," Craig, their oldest said.

"I know you will," she said.

"You'll be fine, this Dr. Campagna sounds like the best," Stan said.

"He is," she said.

"When you get out of here, I'll be the one to take care of you," Steve, the youngest said.

"I have faith in God. Faith in the doctors. And faith in all of you, my precious boys," Marty said. "Now, leave me and your father alone for a minute." The boys gave her hugs and kisses and stepped from the room.

Larry and Marty were left alone in silence.

"Next week, we'll be figuring out how to keep that chestnut wig on my head—you'll have to buy me more fashion hats," she said.

He nodded. He didn't trust himself to speak.

"I love you Lawrence." She hadn't used his proper name since their first meeting.

"I love you Margaret." He was desperate to push the fear from his mind. He needed to be strong for their final kiss before surgery, to give her confidence and reassurance, to show her how much she meant to him. They kissed. It wasn't passion, or strength or any of those things he wanted to give her. But it was love. It had to be enough.

8

Selling Flowers
Medford 1960

Ann stared at the box of assorted yellow, red, and violet plastic flowers. It was one of several boxes that had just arrived. A few months back she had bought several dozen flowers to try out in the store. At first, they were a solid add-on sale or a low cost gift. The store had quickly sold through most of that first purchase order. However, the day Ann reordered, the flowers stopped selling. Ann tried to look on the positive side: they did make the store seem more full.

Lawrence's Jewelers had just moved from the narrow store into a much larger location on the back of the old US Bank building. The scant inventory barely filled the much larger space, necessitating several buying trips to San Francisco. The store grew its on hand selection of high-end merchandise with brands like Kusak Cut Crystal, Castleton China, and Reed and Barton Silver. One wall of the store was covered in clocks. Their medley of ticks and tocks became white noise when the store was empty. Ann's area of responsibility was giftware. She bought statues, crystal and blown glass vases, and on this last trip, too many plastic flowers.

"We'll never be rid of them," Ann told Elsie.

"I'm sure they'll sell," Elsie said.

"These are my smoking jackets," Ann said.

"Smoking jackets?" Elsie wore a bemused smile.

"At the end of World War Two, Neiman Marcus bought enough silk to make hundreds of smoking jackets —the time had past and the jackets were a dud." Ann tossed one of the plastic flowers back into the box. "You poor enthralling flowers, your time has past."

"You got carried away," Elsie said, "we all do."

"It was a mistake to buy so many the second time around. People only want the new and novel," Ann said.

"Like those Kennedy—Nixon debates?" Elsie asked. For the first time in American politics, people could watch the candidates debate live on television.

Ann arranged several of the plastic flowers in a crystal vase. "Speaking of campaigning, a funny thing happened yesterday. I was knocking on doors and a fellow answered and he said, 'If you run, I'll vote for you!'"

Elsie chuckled.

"So I told him: 'Well, thanks a lot, but I'm campaigning for Dick Travis right now!'"

"Maybe you should run for City Council," Elsie said.

Ann had considered running, but only to promote the police and courts. Her parents had been her first influences in politics, leading the then too-young-to-vote Ann to be sick to her stomach when Conservative Candidate Wendell Wilkie lost to Franklin Roosevelt in the 1940 election. After reading Ayn Rand's *Atlas Shrugged*, Ann became an Objectivist. She had a strong belief in laissez-faire government and thought it's only duty was to protect individual rights. She had been to enough City Council meetings to know that's not what happened there.

"How are the boys?" Elsie asked.

Ann blushed. "Jerry tried to visit you last week."

Elsie raised one questioning eyebrow while she added the day's sales receipts into the ledger.

"He got on his tricycle and rode all the way up the street. But you weren't there. This fellow with a pickup brought him back to the house. I was so sick that day I didn't even miss him." Ann managed a weak smile. "I think I got the flu when I took Chuck to Astoria to see his grandmother."

The thought of fried fish and *pulla* sweet bread drizzled with bilberry *kiisseli* made her miss her late husband all over again. Visiting his family was always bitter sweet, but Ann felt Chuck should know where he came from.

Elsie smiled and patted Ann on the back of the hand. "You were always easier than your brother. Boys have a way of getting into trouble. All that aside, I convinced the ladies of Zonta that you would be an excellent addition."

Ann was already involved with P.E.O., currently known as the 'Philanthropic Educational Organization,' the group's original name remains a closely guarded secret known only to members. Ann had joined shortly after her divorce. The support and sisterhood of the group gave her strength to embark on her journey as a single mother. One of the primary goals of the P.E.O. is to assist the advancement of women, particularly those whose education has been interrupted by the needs of supporting a family. Ann began a path of lifelong learning, starting with philosophy and government and growing to include gemology, business, and more.

While P.E.O. gave Ann a strong support network, her friends considered marriage vital to a woman's happiness and often attempted to introduce her to eligible men. Getting attention from men wasn't the problem—her frequent television appearances promoting Lawrence's Jewelers made her a local celebrity.

The problem was that she compared every man she met to her late first husband. Chuck Sr. had died a vibrant youth full of charm, innocence, and a heart full of romance. The middle aged men Ann now met seemed less interested in romance and more in conquest. Ann, not wishing to be viewed this way by men, fully embraced P.E.O. traditions and began to further integrate herself into a culture of liberated female, one who didn't seek to support a man in his success, but instead sought to work side by side with men like an equal.

Once, the jewelry store had been like Ann's husband, something for her to support and care for. Her liberation, however, changed her view of the store. A man might see the business as a sign of his authority, productivity, and success; but Ann followed her mother's strong example, and came to see Lawrence's Jewelers as a family, with her growing into the role of matriarch. She was no longer working at the store because she needed to work there, but instead, because the store needed her to. The store was becoming an extension of herself. She intended to give it every opportunity to succeed.

With a smile, Ann arranged several dozen colorful plastic flowers for the sidewalk sale. She smiled at her mother. "Life's given me some twists, but you and Dad have always been there for me. Now, let's see if we can sell these flowers and make room for something new."

9

The Long Shadow
Medford 1964

Larry barely noticed the mild September sun or the immaculate green grass of the back nine. Waiting at the hospital for Marty to get out of surgery had only made him anxious, so he went to the Country Club for sun, open spaces, and a double round of golf. Every swing was directed by muscle memory and each iron selected by instinct. He kept score the first hole, but lost track midway through the second. Had it been two or three strokes to setup for his approach to the green? Golf wasn't helping. He kept thinking of Marty and her shaved head. Between holes he checked his watch. At the completion of his second round, it was still too early to return to the hospital.

He went home to check on the boys and found them occupied with homework and television. He returned to the hospital to wait in one of the uncomfortable plastic chairs.

The only focus he found was in prayer.

Dr. Byers, the family Physician met with Larry. "She's through surgery. They're moving her to the ICU now."

Larry hastened to her bedside.

She was groggy with the last effects of the anesthesia. She focused on Larry long enough for a smile.

"You were right. You made it." Larry grinned and kissed her. "I love you. The boys are getting along fine. They look forward to you coming home soon."

The nurses shooed Larry from the hospital room. Marty needed her rest. He went home and told the boys she had been awake after her surgery. They ate takeout dinner. The stress of the day overwhelmed Larry and he went to bed early.

He woke to a pounding at the door. It was the next-door neighbor. She said, "I just came from the hospital. Marty's taken a turn for the worse."

Larry called the minister from St. Luke's Methodist Church. Together they arrived at the hospital to pray at Marty's bedside with a laying on of hands. Margaret Cowles Horton died in the early hours of the 25th day of October, 1964.

Larry met with Dr. Campagna.

"The tumor was bigger than we could have expected," Dr. Campagna said. "It was swollen and interwoven throughout her brain. There was nothing to do but close her back up. Even if she had survived, at best, it wouldn't be long before she would be in a vegetative state." Dr. Campagna placed his hand on Larry's shoulder. "There was just nothing we could do."

Larry was devastated. He went home to tell his boys, fighting back tears the entire time. They said a prayer for Marty's soul.

She was buried at Siskiyou Memorial Park.

Larry struggled to leave her grave. Half of him was

gone. She had managed the house, kept the boys in line during the week, been a gracious companion, and always been willing to rough it in the woods or at their simple cabin. Now she was gone and Larry feared he'd never put the pieces of his life back together.

Larry's community of friends rallied in support for those first weeks of mourning. Between the Methodist Church, United Way, the City Planning Commission, and the Kiwanis Club, several home cooked meals were delivered to the house. To supplement this, Larry hired a woman to do cooking and cleaning.

Larry needed a plan to get past his grief. "I can't be sorry for myself." He talked to the wide, blue sky. "Marty, we had a good life together. You're gone now. There's nothing I can do to change that. I have to visualize a life without you until that feels normal."

A rushed return to dating led him to chase the ghost of Marty. He wanted his old life back, with a dedicated homemaker raising the boys. He yearned for their family camping trips and church activities.

After meeting a bevy of women, he ended up sitting with Shirley in Glendale. He thought he might have it all back again. She could raise the boys as effortlessly as Marty had—she even already knew them. But every time he looked at Shirley, and watched her face scrunch in a laugh, Larry realized that while Shirley was familiar, and in that sense comfortable, she would never by Marty.

"Larry…" she smiled. Her smile faltered. "What's wrong?"

"This isn't going to work out."

He and his boys returned home.

Larry lost himself in self-improvement books. While

they helped him improve in dealing with business and social situations, they didn't bring much solace in the area of love. But when he spent time to really reflect, he realized it was simple. He had already met the best woman for him: Ann. He didn't know if would work out —Ann wasn't like the other women in the valley. She made her own mind, and wasn't desperate to settle down.

He went to his office to call her. His hand hesitated over the phone. Larry closed his eyes and took a breath. His hand shook. He had to let go of Marty first.

Over dinner, Craig, his oldest boy said, "I wish I had told mom I loved her before she died."

"She knew," Larry said.

Craig's expression changed from regret to a stoic steadiness. "I still feel her sometimes. I can't explain it, but I truly and deeply believe that she's in the afterlife, blessing and watching over us. She's living in us."

Larry felt that Craig was right, that Marty was still looking down on them, and watching over them from Heaven. He returned to Marty's grave, where a February frost made the grass crunch underfoot. Cold air filled Larry's lungs.

"I need your blessing," he told the tombstone.

Wind rustled the tree leaves. Long morning shadows stretched in bands across the grass hill. He didn't get an answer in words or divine signs, but when he went to call Ann that evening, his hand didn't shake, nor did he feel a surge of adrenaline, but instead he felt a simple rightness in the action.

10

The Noose is Told
Medford 1965

Larry cradled the telephone receiver between his shoulder and ear as he closed his office door to muffle the sounds of Gilligan's Island down the hall. His boys were laughing raucously at the show's hijinks. Good, he thought, they'd be too distracted to interrupt him. He dialed Ann's number.

While he hadn't been nervous to call, now that he heard the ring and waited for an answer, an excitement came over him. Would she answer? Was she out for the evening? He exhaled and tried to pretend he was making a business call.

The phone stopped ringing, and he heard fumbling, then a young voice said, "Hello?"

"Hello, this is Larry Horton calling for Ann."

Larry heard more fumbling, then a thud of the receiver hitting a table. A distant, soft, "Mom!" was heard. Larry waited. More noise.

"This is Ann." Her voice sounded cautious.

"Hi Ann, Larry here, I would like to see you again," he said.

"I'm not sure about that," Ann said.

Larry paused. Since he'd become a widower, available women had been practically throwing themselves at him. "Not sure about what?" he asked.

"You seemed quite popular with the ladies at Kiwanis Kapers and I want you to know I'm not a free love kind of girl." Larry had given Shirley tickets to the event and hadn't realized Ann was in attendance.

"I'm not a guy just looking to score. Of all the women I've met, you're the best. I'd like to get to know you better." He hoped honesty would win her over, but the lingering silence on the other end of the line had him worried.

At length, Ann said, "I'm part of a Great Decisions group. You're welcome to join us."

They got to know each other over discussions of the Vietnam War. The United States Air Force had just begun Operation Rolling Thunder—a series of aerial bombardments against the North Vietnamese that would continue for three and a half years. The group also debated about domestic events like the Selma to Montgomery marches and the now infamous Bloody Sunday that turned global attention towards lingering racial segregation in Alabama.

Each time Larry and Ann met, Larry's reliably moral character whittled away a little more of the baggage from Ann's second marriage, and Larry's somewhat awkward flirtations slowly convinced her that there was a chance that true romance could follow. Ever so slowly Ann thawed from the winter of her passion's isolation to a fresh spring of hope and amour. The season of rebirth led Ann to convince her cousin Nancy Lee to invite Larry and his boys to Easter Dinner.

While Larry had previously met Elsie and Ann's brother Bob at Lawrence's, this was his first meeting with Ann's father, Arnel Butler.

"What do you do?" Larry asked.

"I like to take pictures of wildflowers," Arnel said.

Usually when Larry used his go-to line, people responded with what kind of work they were in which allowed Larry to compartmentalize them into an area of future networking. Larry wasn't sure how to respond to the idea that someone took pictures of wildflowers and all he could think to ask was, "Is there good money in that?"

"No, not really." Arnel said it with an innocent confidence that precluded follow up questions.

A conversational silence formed. Larry scrambled for more topics, eventually saying, "I understand you have a cabin at Diamond Lake."

"I do."

"I have one at Anderson Butte Ridge."

Arnel merely nodded. Larry was having difficulty getting Arnel to open up in conversation. Partially this was due to Arnel's private nature.

Larry wasn't alone in first meetings. His sons and Ann's sons vaguely knew each other from school as Ann's oldest, Chuck was six months younger than Larry's youngest, Steve. Fortunately, the boys got along better than Larry had hoped.

Ultimately, Easter Dinner had been a mixed success. Larry had yet to win over the kind but protective Elsie or the inscrutable Arnel. He was, however, falling for Ann and felt their boys could be brothers.

For her part, Ann reached the same conclusion. Larry

seemed exactly the kind of father her boys needed, one who was stern, kind hearted, and reliable. He was exactly what she had waited for, someone who was honest, earnest, and a fellow deep thinker. Someone she could grow old with. His playful, yet awkward flirtations didn't hurt, either.

It was early June when Larry invited Ann to a romantic dinner. "This Great Decisions group we've been participating in has convinced me we have a great decision to make ourselves. We're both adults so it should be pretty easy to make. Should we get married? You have a decision to make. I have a decision to make—I've already made mine. Ann, you're the lady I want to spend the rest of my life with."

Her first answer was a kiss. Her second: "Yes, Larry, I'll marry you. But aren't you forgetting something?"

"Oh?"

"A ring," Ann teased.

"I don't own a jewelry store," Larry quipped.

This new romance had awoken a verbal trickster in Larry. Shortly after Ann announced the engagement to her Zonta group, an article was published in the Medford Mail Tribune with the headline, 'The News is Told,' describing their engagement. Larry joked to Ann, "The Noose is told!" He put one hand next to his head and lifted it high, tilting his head to the side and miming strangulation by hanging.

Larry's parents, Gene and Retta came to Medford for Father's Day weekend. Larry's parents had been married for over forty years and they brought Kansas pragmatism with them.

"Are you sure about this woman you've been writing us

about?" Gene asked Larry.

"Why yes."

"She has two kids," Gene continued.

"Well, I have three," Larry countered.

"She's been single for how long?" Retta asked.

"Almost eight years now," Larry said.

"That's a long time to be independent," Retta said. "Maybe she won't take to being married."

"Just wait until you meet her," Larry said. He knew the dynamic woman who he had fallen in love with would win them over just as she had won him over. They lunched at Ann's home.

Ann was shy and preferred to let others do the talking. Still, she could hold her own on topics of virtually any subject, and she kept her laugh easy and comfortable, making anyone she met feel like an old friend.

Afterwards, Retta told Larry, "I can see why you like her so much. But this won't be anything like your last marriage."

Meanwhile, Ann's parents were also initially skeptical of the engagement.

"Your mother and I have been talking," Arnel said, "and we think you should sign a prenuptial agreement."

"A prenuptial!" Ann felt a moment of anxiety at how her second marriage had ended. "You don't think it'll last?"

"It's not that," Elsie said, "we just want to keep the store in the family. We want it protected for Bob's kids, and your kids."

The prenuptial was drafted by Ann's brother in-law, signed by Larry and Ann, and promptly forgotten.

Ann and Larry were Married on August 14th, 1965 at

the Episcopal Church in Medford. Both Ann's minister and Larry's Methodist minister officiated. Larry was 40 and Ann was 38.

Their honeymoon began with a flight to Los Angeles where Ann met Larry's brother Dean and his family. They spent the day at the beach.

The two-week honeymoon continued with a flight to Mazatlan, then to Puerto Vallarta. They enjoyed the sights, from the cobblestone city center, to the ornate Nuestra Señora de Guadalupe church, and the beach side promenade. The city was a booming tourist destination from Elizabeth Taylor's recent film, *The Night of the Iguana*. And while Puerto Vallarta is on Mexico's Pacific coast, Larry and Ann failed to realize that it was not in the Pacific Time Zone—the city is roughly due south of Boulder, Colorado. When they went to the airport to catch a plane to Guadalajara, they were late. Their seats had already been sold and the plane left without them.

They didn't make it to Guadalajara until the next morning. The original plan had been to stay with former contacts of Larry's, however, because of the missed flight, there was nobody to pick them up. Not knowing a contact phone number, Larry and Ann had to take a taxi. All they had to go on was an old address. The taxi driver played the part of diligent detective, pursuing leads all over town until he finally found the current home of Larry's friends. The diligent taxi driver beamed with pride. The total charge was $10, about $75 in today's currency.

The next stop on the honeymoon was Mexico City. While eating a lunch of *pechuga adobada*—chicken breast in adobo stock—outside of their hotel, Ann suddenly felt queasy. "I think I might have Montezuma's Revenge."

"I feel it, too," Larry said.

"All the waiters and waitresses are standing in doorways." Ann realized they were in the middle of an earthquake. It was the 7.5 magnitude Oaxaca earthquake that took six lives.

After lunch they went to the Museum of the City of Mexico, located near the site where Hernán Cortés and Moctezuma II met. Dedicated to the history of Mexico from Aztec times to modern day, it planted the first seeds of global travel and culture in an already cosmopolitan Ann.

In the gift shop, Ann noticed a gold coin. "This would look lovely on my bracelet," Ann told Larry.

"It's too expensive," Larry said. Larry held up his billfold. "We don't have many dollars left." General purpose credit cards wouldn't be invented until 1966 when Bank of America established what would eventually become Visa. Travelers had to plan how much cash to take with them or go through the more complicated process of telegram wiring funds. ATM machines were still over fifty years away.

Ann frowned. "Shame. It is a lovely piece."

On the street, musicians played violin. Ann and Larry stopped to enjoy the music. Ann leaned her head on Larry's shoulder. "I'm really enjoying this," she said.

"They're selling records over there. We have enough dollars for that."

"Not the music—well the violins are nice—but I mean this honeymoon." Ann smiled.

"Let's buy the record. So we can remember." Larry put his arm around her. For the moment they were lost in the soaring harmonies as two violin melodies formed a duet that rose and fell, always coming back to join again and again in building surges towards a seemingly forever distant crescendo. They listened to the music, happy and content, and very much filled with love as they enjoyed the magic of their new romance and life together.

11

Moving In
Medford 1965

Upon return from their honeymoon, Ann and Larry undertook the task of moving Ann's household into the larger house at 509 North Barneburg where their three cars filled the driveway: Larry's 1965 four-door, straight-stick Chevrolet, Ann's blue Volkswagen Bug, and Craig's small Renault.

Chuck and Jerry helped unload the moving truck.

"We're not going to be Wirkkulas anymore, we're all Hortons now," Ann said. "You boys have a father now. That's something special."

"I've been praying for a Dad," Jerry said.

Inside, Ann asked Larry, "Should we move Chuck and Jerry into the third upstairs bedroom?"

"That's my office," Larry said.

"Well, yes," Ann said. "You could move your office to the basement so everyone could be on the same floor."

Larry opened the door to his office so Ann could see just how monumental a task it would be to move Larry's office. Every horizontal surface was covered with well-organized stacks of Electrical Engineering plans, text books, and correspondence while a free-range collection of architectural and electrical drawings covered walls and other surfaces. Most importantly, however, the room had one of the only two air conditioning units in the house, a window unit that allowed Larry to continue working during the heat of summer. "I've always worked two jobs. At the power company and my consulting job. That's how I got this big house. This room has always been set aside for drafting and engineering. It's probably doubled my income."

"I have money coming in from the store," Ann said.

"Well, yes." Larry looked at his coveted office, the back to Ann. "I'll keep the office. It'll be too much disruption to move it. Because of the extra income, I can pay the rent and utilities and replace the cars, and pay for the boy's expenses. You can buy the groceries and your own clothes and gas."

"That all seems fine," Ann said, "but what do we do with the boys?"

"Stan and Craig can live in the basement—they're hardly home anymore anyway. The younger three can stay in the back bedroom," Larry said.

Hot August nights set upon Medford. One evening after work, Ann caught Chuck, Jerry, and Steve hovering outside of Larry's office. They had cracked the door as far as they dared so that a cool breeze could blow from the air conditioning into the hallway. When they saw Ann, they quickly closed the door and scampered past her and out to the backyard. One of the most important rules of the house was to never disturb Larry while he was working.

On Ann's way to the kitchen, she noticed that the nude statue—a woman, ten-inch plaster of paris—had been turned so the back faced the room. Ann corrected the statue back to face the room, chuckling to herself at the cleaning lady's modest persistence at turning the statue around.

While everyone was on their own for breakfast and lunch, Ann assumed the duty of preparing the family's evening meal. The Great Decisions group that Ann and Larry had participated in gave them a bunch of cans, minus the labels, as a wedding present. The mystery ingredient was supposed to anchor the meal—pork and beans, green beans, pears—whenever Ann came across an ingredient she didn't know how to utilize she resorted to her go-to meal: jambalaya. Anything could be mixed with meat, vegetables, and rice. Add to that, potatoes and gravy, macaroni and cheese, and frequent peanut butter and jam rolls. Everything that growing boys needed.

Ann began to suspect she got the bad end of the deal with Larry, as five teenage boys could eat a lot of food. An eight-pound roast—gone. A five-pound bag of potatoes, mashed up with butter—gone. Two gallons of milk delivered every other day—gone. A dozen eggs scrambled in the morning—gone. Frequently, the last boy to the kitchen got a meager portion and had to pass his plate around the table so everyone else could donate a little food back to him. The food bill was often staggering, and usually in excess of mortgage and utilities. One thing that helped Ann was renting out her old house.

"How does it feel to be a landlord?" Larry asked her.

"I'm very fortunate. The couple I got is great. They're cleaning the place up better than I did. The yard looks fantastic," Ann said.

When the snows came, the family took up winter sports.

Ann and her boys were comfortable on ice and snow— Arnel continued to be an avid outdoorsman and had helped Ann teach both the boys the keys to success on skates and skies. Jerry, the youngest boy, particularly took to skiing.

While snow sports were popular with the family, it rarely snowed on the valley floor. It did that winter, however. Ann hit ice on her way downtown to pickup Craig from the auto dealership where he was having his car serviced. Her car skidded slowly towards another car. There was nothing for Ann to do but grip the steering wheel and wait. The steel cars bumped against each other. Fortunately, there wasn't a dent to either car. When Ann reached the dealership, neither Craig nor his car were there. Ann found a payphone and dialed Larry, who knew the address of the mechanic where Craig had gone. By the time Ann reached the mechanic, Craig had already walked in the snow from downtown to school.

It was one of many times where Craig demonstrated a fierce self-reliance. While Larry attempted to furnish college tuition for the boys, Craig managed to pay his own way through a year at Willamette and three at the University of Oregon by joining the Merchant Marines to sail the Pacific Ocean on tankers and freighters.

At the time Ann and Larry married, Ann had been a lifelong Episcopalian and Larry a lifelong Methodist. They alternated Sundays between the Episcopalian and Methodist churches.

"I don't feel like a very good church goer anymore," Ann said.

"Oh?" Larry asked.

"It's the annual pledge. I guess I got a little scotch on

my money. Two churches…double the tithe," Ann said.

"We pick one church then," Larry said.

"Which one? The Methodist church feels too casual," Ann said.

"The Episcopalian church feels too formal," Larry said.

They were at an impasse.

"If we can't decide on a church, what are we going to do?" Larry asked.

"Did you finish *Atlas Shrugged*?"

"Well, yes."

"She wasn't one for church, but for individual empowerment."

"What about God?" Larry asked.

"We don't have to give up on God." Ann had already made her peace with reconciling Ayn Rand's philosophy with her belief in God. Sometimes Ann wondered if Ayn Rand's atheism was a result of her upbringing in Russia at the time of the Communist Revolution. Ann, like many Americans of the 1960s had come to fear the Communist menace. Works like Freda Utley's *The China Study* portrayed a Capitalist Chiang Kai-shek pitted against the Communist Mao Tse-tung. Senator McCarthy's Red Scare was still fresh on everyone's minds and the Cold War was far from over. But for Ann, the belief of individual empowerment could be thought as an extension of God's will. "Things turn out for the best for some reason, and I'll attribute that to God," she surmised.

"What are we going to do to substitute for attendance?" Larry couldn't imagine camping as their sole tradition. As much as he liked the outdoors, he also appreciated the feeling of belonging that a church gave.

"I'm sure we'll think of something," Ann said.

12

Whisper on the Wind
Southern Oregon 1966

Newlyweds Ann and Larry continued to acclimate to their Brady Bunch like household. While work kept Ann and Larry busy during the week, their weekends in the large, empty house were dull.

"We could try golf," Larry suggested.

Ann agreed. They started with a late morning round. Dew on the grass soaked through Ann's shoes. She sloshed through the course. By the fourth hole, her feet were cold, wet, and numb.

"We have a group coming up behind us," Larry said.

Ann looked over her shoulder: not just a group, but four golfers. Her and Larry were slower than a group of four. Maybe not Larry. Maybe just her.

"Come on, quickly, they're waiting," Larry said.

Ann studied the ball and the lurking green. She readied her seven iron. A quick back-swing, a solid hit and the ball soared high. Too high. It plunked into the tall grass on the far side of the green.

"This really isn't any fun," Ann said.

"What isn't fun about this?" Larry asked.

"I'm cold. My feet are wet. What a miserable day." Ann shook the seven iron at the fogged over sky.

Later, as they warmed over coffee, Larry said, "We need something to do."

"Father's cabin has always been fun," Ann said. "He even bought a new toy—a boat."

Larry raised an eyebrow.

Diamond Lake was a two-hour drive to the north. The cabin was on the West Rim. They found the small plastic boat stored in a shed. It had a removable mast and keel outboards.

They launched the boat. With the wind behind them, they raced down the lake. Ann found an eager happiness on the water. The wind, the cold of the lake, the deep blue of the sky, the serenity, everything was like a dream.

The return trip was more of a challenge.

"We could row." Ann fingered the oars.

"Let's master the wind," Larry said.

It took them time to learn to sail into the wind, and their return to the cabin took several hours…and a few choice applications of the oars. When they docked the boat, Larry said simply, "I'm hooked."

Through a social contact, Larry learned that the local Boy Scout Troop received a grant to buy larger sailboats. He told Ann, "We could get one at their group rate."

Ann agreed. $600 later they had a 14-foot C-Lark.

"It has a nice blue stripe," Ann said of the boat.

The C-Lark was more complicated than the plastic dinghy. Neither of them knew what to do with it. Ann's brother Bob volunteered to teach them to sail. The trio went to Emigrant Lake in late autumn 1968 and launched the boat on a brisk afternoon.

"Those clouds look ominous," Ann said.

"We'll be fine," Bob said. From a man who once drove a snowmobile across Diamond Lake during the spring thaw, this was hardly a relief to Ann.

"Here's what you need to know about sailing," Bob said. "First, this is the boom. It holds the bottom of the mainsail." He demonstrated how it would swing back and forth.

"Why do they call it the boom?" Ann asked.

"If you don't pay attention: BOOM." He mimed the boom striking the side of his head. "Avoid that. Right now, we're in the cockpit." He pointed at the open-to-the-air benches they sat on. While pulling a teak handle back and forth, he said, "This is the rudder controller. The tiller. It turns the boat." He pointed to the mast. "You have a sloop configuration. That means you have a mainsail to catch wind and really move, and a jib sail to cut down on turbulence."

"Cut down on turbulence?" Larry asked.

"You want your main sail to stay full all the time," Bob said. "The jib is there to cut the air." He held one hand straight up and down and curved the fingers of his other hand slightly in front. "It guides air around the main sail so you don't lose your wind. They call it the Venturie effect."

Larry nodded.

Bob tapped his foot on a strap that ran across the floor of the cockpit. "This is your hiking strap. Hook your feet under it so you can lean against the wind. Your weight keeps the boat upright, so the sail can stay full."

"You mean lean over the edge of the boat?" Ann asked.

"Well, yes. If you don't, then the wind will push your

sail over and you'll lose speed. Lastly you need to know about the jib. The jib is strung up on the front stay by sheets."

Ann looked around. "I just see the sail."

"The ropes on the sails are called sheets." Bob wiggled one. "The rest of the ropes are called lines." He slid to the front of the boat. "You use cam cleats to keep the jib sheet tight." He pulled the line running from the edge of the jib and locked it into the cleat. "Now we're ready to sail."

They put from shore. The boat accelerated once it reached open water.

"We're really going!" Ann said.

"Once we get away from the shore—the trees—we can really pick up speed," Bob said. "One of you get on the hiking strap. The wind is starting to push us over."

Ann and Larry exchanged a glance.

"One of us needs to learn to captain," Larry said without budging from his seat next to the tiller.

"Fine. I'll be the crew," Ann said. She crawled to the edge of the cockpit, put her feet into the hiking straps as Bob had demonstrated, grabbed the teak handrails, and leaned over the water. The boat slowly righted and Ann felt the sloop gain speed. Water blurred by her peripheral vision. She didn't dare to look directly at it. Icy water splashed at her cheeks. Her heartbeat rushed and only calmed again when something white and puffy whirled past. She leaned back into the boat. "It's snowing."

"Why would it be..." Larry trailed off. He looked to the sky. One of his hands was on the tiller. He held his other out to catch a snowflake. "It is." He laughed.

After taking lessons from the Rogue Yacht club, Ann

and Larry signed up for competition. Their first race was in late July at Howard Prairie Lake for the Rogue Yacht Club's annual regatta. Wind blew from north by northwest —essentially straight down the narrow lake. By following the wind, the course was a two and a half nautical mile sprint.

When the red flag with white dot was raised and the airhorn sounded, Larry and Ann sailed their blue-striped C-Lark towards the starting line. A blue flag with a white interior rectangle was raised and again the airhorn sounded.

"Four minutes to start," Larry said.

"We're going to get there before everyone else," Ann said.

The other four C-Larks were still significantly up-wind.

The airhorn sounded again and the blue flag lowered.

"One minute to start." Larry sounded nervous.

"We're going too fast! We're going to cross the start early!" Ann realized.

"Lower the sail!" Larry started a series of s-curves that killed their speed and kept them behind the starting line when the final airhorn sounded. Unfortunately, the maneuver also left them dead in the water. The other boats that had been farther up-wind clipped by at top speed.

As they crossed the starting line, Larry muttered, "We blew it." The other boats were far enough ahead that they couldn't possibly catch up.

Their next regatta was at Tenmile Lake, near Lakeside, Oregon, north of Coos Bay.

Ann walked along the dock while Larry launched their boat. Guiding the boat into the water took all of Ann's attention and she didn't notice one of the dock boards was missing. Her foot slipped into the gap. She fell, smacking her knee on the next board.

"Is the boat in the water?" Larry yelled.

Ann hobbled back to her feet. Her knee bled and throbbed with pain. "The boat's fine!" she yelled back.

Larry and Ann boarded their boat and sailed towards the starting line. This time, they kept back. When the final flag lowered and a single shotgun blast sounded, signaling the start of their race; they were close to top speed with Ann secure in her hiking straps, leaning over the side of the boat, to keep the sail catching as much wind as possible.

The race was a simple triangle with four legs and three marker buoys. They overshot the turn on the first marker and were in second place coming into the next marker. The wind was at their sail. Ann leaned back enough to feel water spray on her cheeks.

"Larry, he's leeward!" Ann yelled. "He has the right-of-way."

"I can squeeze past him," Larry yelled back.

"You're going to hit him!"

"It's called aggressive sailing!" Larry kept the boat on course while the gap between the lead boat and the marker buoy narrowed.

Ann, half of her body hanging over the side of the boat, couldn't do anything but strain against the foot straps to keep her body rigid. Her injured knee buckled. She slipped. *Don't go overboard*, she thought. Her hands gripped the railing. She looked up. The other boat had come to an almost complete stop at the marker.

"Larry!"

"Brace for impact!"

Ann and Larry's blue striped boat collided with the red bottomed C-Lark ahead of them. Impact rocked their boat. Ann inhaled as she got dunked. Icy water poured into her lungs. She broke the surface of the lake in a coughing fit.

"Get in the boat!" Larry yelled.

Ann continued to cough.

"Get in the boat!" Larry repeated.

Fortunately, Ann still had a grip on the jib sheet and she pulled her way to the boat and hauled herself over the gunwale and landed in the open cockpit with a wet *splosh*. She wiped sodden strands of hair from her face.

"Enjoy your pair of dots!" The skipper of the other boat yelled.

"Let's undo the penalty," Ann said.

Hitting another boat required 'a pair of dots,' named for a maneuver performed by circling a marker twice in penalty. Each lap of the buoy required two tacks—sailing into the wind—and two jibs—sailing with the wind behind. As they completed the penalty, Ann realized what had happened to them: "That jut stole the other boat's wind." She pointed at a tree-covered arm of land.

They finished the race last.

Ann dried her hair. "Well, we blew that race."

Larry laughed.

"What's so funny?"

"You said you gave up golf because you didn't want to be wet and miserable."

"I might be wet, but I'm not miserable." Ann joined his laugh.

A string of early failures led to naming the blue-striped

boat, *Bluit*. During the off season, Ann and Larry took classes, private lessons, read books on racing, and shopped for an upgraded boat.

"This one," Ann suggested. It was white on top and solid blue from the gunwale down.

"Sure." It met with Larry's racing specifications. "What should we call it?"

"*Blue Air*." Ann dramatically spread her hands to the sky.

"Are you talking about the noise the skipper makes on the water?" Larry asked, indicating that he frequently blew-air—when he got excited, he shouted. After more than one race, fellow competitors had asked Ann why Larry was so mad. Her default response was that he wasn't angry, just spirited.

By their third season, they mastered the rules of racing, sharpened their on-the-water skills, and learned to tune the boat for optimal performance. During pre-season practice, Larry remarked, "I'm beginning to get the same feel of sailing as I do in flying. Sure it's only a two dimensional plane, but you can go anywhere you want." It was a freedom from terrain that couldn't be matched on land.

They began to dominate the local competition, wracking up wins at Lake of the Woods, Howard Prairie, Klamath Lake, Fern Ridge Reservoir, Lake Port, the Columbia River and Eureka. The wins earned them a spot at the state championship in Eugene where they qualified for the gold medal race.

The course consisted of two laps around four markers before crossing the finish line along the windward direction. Larry timed their approach to the starting line.

They were at maximum speed as the starting gun fired.

During leeward legs, they jibed back and forth in a zig-zag pattern, keeping their boat on a broad reach with the wind coming from hard starboard or port tack. By doing this instead of running directly with the wind, the tiller kept more feedback and the boat effectively planed across the surface of the water like a surfboard.

On their final downwind leg, they were in second.

"Luff him! Steal his wind!" Ann's body was stretched taught as she leaned parallel to the water.

Larry kept a steady hand on the tiller. As their sail began to block the wind from the leader, Larry watched the lead boat lose its edge. Its current tack sent it jibing right in front of them. Larry pulled the tiller to cut across the other boat's wake.

"Hold on!"

The wake made their boat bounce and skid. Ann's feet seated deep under the hiking straps and her hands burned as she gripped the teak handrails. She held her breath and closed her eyes as she was doused by wake. When she dared open her eyes again, the water whipped by under her. She was still attached to the boat.

"Keep that vigor!" Larry yelled.

They slipped past the lead boat, taking right of way around the final marker. They tacked windward towards the finish line. Larry kept the boat on edge to maximize speed. Their aggressive maneuver put them half a leg ahead of the other boats.

The wind shifted. *Blue Air* went over. Ann fell backwards into the icy water. The boat came over with her. The C-Lark was small, and just a pair of kicks got Ann free. She breached the surface of the lake to see Larry standing on the boat's keel.

"Quick! We have to right it!" Larry yelled.

Ann grabbed the side of the boat. They leaned together until the boat righted. Larry scrambled and kept dry. He hauled Ann back into the cockpit. Ann bailed water while Larry found the wind.

The second place boat they had luffed was gaining on them.

"We're not missing a place for that capsize!" Larry yelled.

It was a two boat sprint for the finish. With every gust of wind, Ann feared they'd topple back to the water. The other boat backed off, apparently intimidated by the fierce gusts. Larry put *Blue Air* back on edge and kept it there until they crossed the finish line. First.

Ann wrung out her clothes while Larry shook water out of one of his shoes.

"Are you okay?" Larry asked.

Ann's waterlogged scowl flipped to a wicked smile. She jumped into his arms, knocking the both of them overboard.

They surfaced. "What did you do that for? I kept dry!" Larry said.

"We won! We're state champions!" She gave him watery kisses.

Their victory at the Oregon Championship earned them an entry in the National Championships at Fort Ludlow on Puget Sound. Larry showed Ann the rankings. "We're considered among the top eighteen sailors west of the Mississippi for Working Sails Class."

The regatta would be decided by three races. The first day had uncommonly low wind, an effect of the stifling heat in the San Juan Islands.

"Call it a drifter," Larry said. The wind was so low they relied solely on tide energy to keep them moving towards the markers.

Without wind, there was no need for Ann to hike over the hull of the ship. Instead, she stood lookout next to the mast. "There!" She pointed to a green and yellow striped sail. "Looks like the top rated guy got into backwater."

"Is there a way around?" Larry asked.

Ann scanned the water. "I see puffs." Intermittent spray from high-pressure gusts. "There, on the side of the course." Each wind gust propelled them past the drifting boats.

"That was the leader!" Ann yelled. "This is the most exciting thing ever!"

Larry grinned. They finished first.

While the first race had been a drifter, the wind returned for the next two races. The competition was fierce. By the conclusion of the regatta, Ann and Larry finished fourth overall for the West Coast.

13

Self-Help
Medford 1967

Pacific Power wanted to increase Larry's salary. Unfortunately, it came with a catch. They were going to close the Medford office and relocate him to Portland. The move would force Ann to leave Lawrence's, a decision Larry couldn't take lightly. "If I quit the power company, I'll still have my engineering contracts," Larry said. He was under contract to complete Electrical Engineering specifications for Ashland's junior high and high school.

They had two options, to move to Portland and let Larry support the family with a larger salary, or remain in Medford on the combined incomes of Larry's engineering contracts and the store profits. "It's a toss up—we lose income either way," Ann said.

At the power company Larry had spoken before professional engineering organizations, been published in trade journals, and even mentored apprentice engineers. Yet his career with the power company advanced at the same rate as many of his peers who were less distinguished in the field. The limitations of corporate structure were in direct opposition to Larry's visualization techniques. He knew that once he had a clear goal—to generate wealth—he could map a strategy to reach that goal. Once that strategy was in place, Larry was willing to work as hard as necessary to succeed. What he needed to do was to put the theory into practice.

"I'm going to work for myself," he told Ann.

They stayed in Medford. The first several months were slow going. Utilizing his contracts, he had enough income to break even on the rent. This wasn't the future of success he envisioned. He was split in his decision between pursuing the independent path and taking on work so that he could continue to provide a comfortable income to the family. He decided to send letters around the Rogue Valley looking for other income or even salaried work. Southern Oregon University picked him up as a drafting teacher for three years.

His big break came when he was offered a position with Ramic Corporation, a small electronics company working with photo cells. He decided to take the position—but it came with a catch.

"You got to buy twenty-thousand in stock if you want to be an employee in the company," the boss told him.

At the power company, Larry had participated with the employee stock purchase plan whenever possible. It was a lesson that had been deeply ingrained in Larry from his self-help books: accumulate wealth. Being asked to buy stock upfront seemed odd to Larry, but it was also an opportunity to buy into the profits he would bring to the company. He took out a $20,000 loan from the bank against his existing engineering contracts.

A loan meant Larry began accruing interest. Before too much could accumulate, Larry knew he had to finish his contracts so he could pay off the loan. Unfortunately, it was more work than he could complete in a timely fashion. After weighing the options, he decided to hire his first employee, a draftsman who could deliver final drawings on Larry's specifications and sketches. His contracts were completed in prompt succession, and Larry was able to pay off the loan, making him the outright owner of his Ramic stock.

Ramic's primary invention was a machine that could scan plywood for defects. Larry assisted with developing the electronics for the machine. Things went well for the first couple of years, however, in 1969, Ramic's manager was fired for dipping into the till. His replacement met with Larry, and told him, "It says on your resume that you used to work for Finzer's business machines, and that you have some sales experience."

While they were both accurate statements, Larry was in fact not a salesman, something he was quick to point out.

"You've just sold the wrong product." The manager wouldn't budge on his stance.

After a few weeks of sales, Larry told Ann, "I've decided to leave Ramic. I can see they're starting to go downhill. I should get out when I can."

"What about your stock?" Ann asked.

"I'll take out an ad in the paper," Larry said. His add read as follows: 'Wanting to trade $32,000 in Ramic stock for real-estate or cash.'

The lawyer for Ramic contacted Larry. "I saw your ad in the paper. You shouldn't be doing things like that."

"Well, what else am I going to do?" Larry asked.

The lawyer didn't have any ideas. "I'll ask around, see what we can come up with."

Ramic's investors bought the stock back at Larry's cost. At the age of 43, Larry received a massive lump sum of cash worth approximately the equivalent of $200,000 in 2017 dollars. He needed some way to invest it. All of the books that Larry had read on investing stressed the importance of diversification. He put some of the money into the stock market and looked for real estate purchases that would turn the rest of the money into an investment.

Doyle Green had an idea. Doyle was one of the first people Larry had met after moving to Medford. They were both members of the Methodist Church at that time. Doyle was working as a contractor in Ashland, building houses. His idea was simple, "Why don't you buy this lot? It's an acre of land and a house right next to Southern Oregon College. You can make money renting the house."

A few months later, the next house in the development was complete. Doyle called Larry to suggest, "Why don't you buy that one too?"

Larry did. Using a combination of his Ramic buyout as down payment and loans from the bank, Larry was able to buy two houses on adjoining lots for a total investment of $26,000.

Yet Larry had a vision of much more wealth than this and explained it to Ann, "Making wealth is about doing it on a quiet basis over a long period of time. There is no get-rich-quick, just a series of incremental steps towards greater wealth. The important thing is to always build upon what came before."

"What's the next step?" Ann asked.

"About that." Larry grinned. "What are you doing tomorrow?"

14

First Apartment
Medford 1969

Larry shielded his eyes from the morning sun while Ann fanned herself. The previous day's heat had only partially escaped during the night and the day started out hot. From the corner of 4th and Rose, the five-unit apartment looked like an oversized two-story house. All of the units rented with outdated and worn furniture. A 1960s Ford Falcon was the only car still parked on the paved lot that had once been a backyard.

"It looked old when Bob and Alpha Jane lived here." Ann's brother and his wife had lived in these apartments several years ago. Even then Ann had not been impressed.

"It'll keep me out of mischief." In addition to yard work and visible wear, Larry assumed there were other things that would need updating from time to time.

"You've already decided?"

Larry nodded. When he ran into Bob Barbee during a weekend getaway to Diamond Lake, the two had initially reminisced about their time at Pacific Power and Light before Bob had mentioned he had property for sale. Larry quickly studied the opportunity.

"He's asking twenty-five thousand for it," Larry told Ann.

"Did you have any Ramic money left?" Ann asked.

The money from selling off his Ramic stocks had been diversified into other stocks, mutual funds, and the two rental houses in Ashland. While he could liquidate one or more of those to come up with the money, he had a better idea.

"He only needs five-thousand down. We can get a loan for that," he said. "The units rent for seventy-five each. The whole place brings in three-seventy-five a month. We'll pay off the loan in no-time. Five years tops."

Money from rents was enough to pay taxes, mortgage, and upkeep, with money left over in the form of positive cashflow. Additionally, there was a tax benefit from depreciation. As all structures have a useful lifespan, the gradual loss in value can be written off on taxes as a value loss against future sales. This left more positive cashflow for other investments.

Larry was right about the apartments keeping him busy during the weekends. Between filling vacancies, collecting rent, and dealing with deterioration and vandalism, managing the apartments soon took all his free time, including a morning call about broken laundry facilities.

Larry went to the apartments to inspect the damage. Beer bottles were strewn through the lawn. He sniffed the air and smelled the pungent reek of vomit baking in the early morning heat. Downstairs, he found the coin-operated washer and dryer had been broken open, the money he needed to pay utilities was gone. He also found several empty bottles in the washing machine. He started knocking on doors to see what had happened.

"It's that new tenant. She threw a big beer party," one of the residents said.

Larry knocked on her door.

She answered. Her eyes were bloodshot and bleary as she squinted at Larry.

"Did you throw a party last night?" Larry asked.

"Yeah."

"Hey, there are damages," Larry said.

"Not my problem."

It wasn't the answer Larry wanted to hear. His response was quick: "You need to get off these premises." She didn't.

The next morning, when Larry went to go to work, he discovered the upholstery in his car had been cut and ripped by a knife. Suspecting that it was the work of the problem tenant, he knew he needed to apply pressure to someone with influence over the tenant.

Her rental application listed her father as reference. He was a prominent plumber in town. Larry visited him, demanding, "She has to go. This is beyond the norm for any tenant."

The pressure worked, and the father agreed to move his daughter out of the apartment.

Five years later, he had an opportunity to sell the property at a $10,000 profit to a lawyer in Tacoma. The extra after-hours work had left Larry tired of the property, and he took the opportunity for a private-party sale. Instead of getting his money back all at once, payments would be made over-time, so Larry could maintain the positive cashflow the rental had established.

He hired an attorney to draft the sales contract. For three months, all was well. Then payments stopped and the property was soon in default. Several months later, Ann and Larry started the foreclosure process.

"Twenty-two hundred dollars to get it back in our name," Larry said over dinner. They were eating Polynesian Peach Chicken at a small table in the living room. After four of their boys had left for college, the formal dining table seemed too big for the two of them. Besides, the living room had a small color television which currently showed Bob Schieffer reading the news.

"It's a shame. He seemed like a good fellow," Ann said.

"There goes doubling our investment," Larry said.

"At least we got a story out of it. A guy comes to town looking to buy apartments, then poof, vanishes." Ann laughed.

Always looking for opportunity, Larry had a flash of inspiration. "I wonder if he bought more apartments?"

His hunch was right, the lawyer had owned two other properties in Southern Oregon, one in Ashland, and the second in Medford. The one in Medford was an eight-plex. The first mortgage plus liens were close to the assessed value of the property. Larry had identified an opportunity, now he had to follow through on it.

Larry and Ann added their lien to the property, to recoup lost income from the previous default. The apartments went to foreclosure on the courthouse steps. To get it in their name, Larry and Ann had to pay off all of the lien holders, including covering back payments and interest to the first mortgage. The property was secured for $65,000 and reassessed later that year at a value of $95,000. Larry's borrowing power was increased substantially. With another small step towards wealth finished, he began looking for new opportunities.

15

Interlude in the City
San Francisco 1968

Ann and Elsie frequented the San Francisco gift show as buyers for Lawrence's Jewelers. Before Ann and Larry met, Ann wasn't able to leave Chuck and Jerry at home for the several days of the buying trip, so she would bring them along. Gift shows held little appeal to the youngsters, and Elsie made it worth their while by taking them to a San Francisco Giants baseball game every year. On one occasion, Larry was scheduled to be in town completing an Electrical Engineering examination. This gave Ann an opportunity to take Larry to the show and he could see her at work.

They attended a party for an established dinnerware company. Since Ann had started buying for Lawrence's, she tried to diversify the inventory. While the store had a strong selection of fine china, it was lacking in everyday dining options.

"This is a nice party," Larry said.

"We're at a trade show, they're all nice parties," Ann said.

There was a plink from Larry's glass.

"Was that ice cracking?" he asked.

"Look at the bottom of your glass."

A large crack had spread across the base. "It's not leaking," Larry said.

"They must have done something wrong at the factory," Ann said.

As they walked around the party, they heard occasional *plinks*.

"There goes another one," someone muttered.

Still, Ann found the style to be charming. The sales representative convinced her that these were just proof of concept glasses and that the final product wouldn't have this thermal shock flaw. Ann knew the product would sell so long as the final quality was there. She agreed to buy a limited quantity so she could put the final product to the test herself. True to the salesman's word, the defects were gone from the final product.

"How do you pick what you're going to buy?" Larry asked.

"The salesmen are all very good here. That makes it more difficult to tell the right thing to buy. As long as I like it, and I could see myself buying it, I figure someone else in town would like it too," Ann said.

When they met up with Elsie, Chuck and Jerry at the motel after the game, Jerry yelled, "Grandma caught a foul ball! She closed her eyes and it just landed in her hand!"

Elsie showed them the ball as proof.

Several years later, with Larry's encouragement, Ann began to attend the Los Angeles gift show. There, instead of dinners, the vendors hosted their potential clients for breakfast. Hollywood talent was often the entertainment. Some of the more memorable performers were comedian Phyllis Diller and Cal Worthington, a Los Angeles car salesman made famous for his antic filled television commercials.

While Larry attended the breakfasts with Ann, one day on the gift show floor was enough for him, and he opted out of the second day with a mischievous, "I'll find something to do." A wink implied he already had something in mind.

Over dinner, they compared notes on the day.

"That show Roots got me thinking," Larry said. "What are my roots? I spent the day at the Los Angeles county library. I didn't find anything on my family, but I found a lot about yours."

The day at the gift show had left Ann's head full of china patterns, crystal sculptures, and decorative clocks. Genealogy was an unexpected dinner topic.

"Well, what did you find?" Ann asked.

"The first Lawrences came from Switzerland."

It was one possible explanation for the family's tradition of watch making and it seeded an idea. Ann would expand Lawrence's assortment of designer watches. They already had the best watch repairman in town—her brother. Including the best selection of watches in the region seemed an ideal fit for the store.

They returned to Medford, and soon Ann's new purchase orders began arriving. As Ann was arranging a new display of crystal near the front door, Bob came over to admire the new pieces.

"I really like that instead of just selling jewelry, we have housewares. It's helped us make a unique store," he said.

Ann's efforts had grown the gift sales to be nearly on par with the jewelry sales, with most of the customers coming to buy gifts.

As usual with new items, Ann's recent purchases didn't immediately fly off the shelves. Because Ann bought directly from the Los Angeles gift shows, she often had products before shoppers even knew to look for them. Customer education was an ongoing struggle.

One woman was looking over a crystal figurine when she exclaimed, "I bought this in San Francisco last week!"

"It's been right there longer than that," Ann said with a laugh. Small town shoppers had been habituated to think that anything new and interesting must be in San Francisco first, a false assumption Ann had been working hard to correct.

"Is there anything I can help you with?" Ann asked the shopper who shook her head no.

"I'm waiting for the young man," the shopper said.

"I'm sure I can help you with whatever you need," Ann said.

"I don't mind waiting."

There were three other women waiting to be helped by the young male clerk. Even though Ann had picked most of the merchandise in the store, giving her a deep understanding of the product, many customers preferred to buy from a man.

Ann tried to keep busy cleaning china. She watched as the clerk helped the ladies one at a time, finally taking the last lady, the shopper from San Francisco, to the watch cabinet. After a couple minutes there, they went to Bob at the repair bench. Bob simply pointed to Ann.

The young clerk brought the lady over. He said, "Ann,

she wants to buy a popular watch for her husband, but I don't know anything about them."

Ann smiled inside. The lady could have saved several minutes just by letting Ann help her to begin with.

"This is the one that I was thinking of getting him." The woman pointed to a common, round-faced goldplate Seiko watch. "Is it popular? My husband goes to San Francisco for business. He needs to look trendy."

The watch the woman wanted was an older style that had been around for years. Popular, yes; trendy, no.

"This is the one you want to get him, an Omega Seamaster Swiss Quartz watch." Ann directed the woman's attention to a square faced stainless steel watch. "It's just come out and is all the rage in Los Angeles."

"I thought watches were supposed to be round!" the woman exclaimed.

"They should have these in San Francisco any day now." Ann smiled. She had only received the watch earlier that day.

"Well, I don't know," the woman hesitated. "I suppose I'll have to wait and ask him what's popular down there these days."

Ann felt herself cringe. Later, she commiserated with Elsie.

"I had the Seiko sold if I hadn't kept talking—the woman wasn't ready for something new." Ann shook her head. "Just wrap it up and sell it."

"Sometimes we learn things the hard way," Elsie said. "You seem to be getting the hang of this buying—usually a step ahead of the trends. The customers will figure that out as well. They'll come around." Elsie shared her warm smile with Ann.

16

Something Out of Nothing
Medford 1969

"I heard from Craig," Larry told Ann over breakfast. "He's decided not to finish the insurance training." Craig, instead, enlisted in the Navy. Larry had gotten lucky when he enlisted—the war ended while he was still in training. While the war was starting to wind down through the process of Vietnamization, there were still Americans in combat, which made for the very real chance that Craig would see action.

Larry shook his head and scratched at the itch forming on the back of his neck. "I shouldn't worry about things I can't change. Just those I can. Maybe I won't feel so... restless. We're both self-employed. We need to be better prepared for retirement than we are," Larry said.

"Isn't that why you're investing in the stock market?"

Larry showed Ann the morning's Wall Street Journal. He had been tracking several stocks every morning for the past year. "Everything's down, again." The stock market had peaked mid 1969, at the same time he bought. From there, the stock market tumbled, losing 50% of its value by 1970. "I sold Lockheed today, four dollars a share,"

Larry said.

"Didn't you buy that for sixteen?"

"Inflation's getting bad. Stocks aren't turning around. I wanted to get something back," Larry said. Rampant inflation continued until the mid-eighties when the stock market finally began to recover. Larry and Ann shifted to a buy and hold strategy, keeping among others, Raytheon, Boeing, and Alcoa.

Larry also attempted to earn money on commodities but soon found the market to be uncomfortably volatile. Commodity values ticked up and down all day long. Larry would be up a thousand, then down a thousand.

"I keep losing sleep," he confessed to Ann. "The not knowing…is it going up? Going down? Then I get nervous and generally do the opposite of what I should do."

"You made money in coffee and sugar didn't you?"

"And lost more in wheat, corn, and soybeans." Larry folded the paper and put it aside.

While the stock market had yet to pay any reasonable dividends, Larry's property investments continued to thrive. The rental properties paid for themselves and offered advantageous tax breaks. Structural depreciation and other deductions allowed Larry to take a business loss on his taxes, reducing the taxes owed and freeing that capital for further investment.

"There's a downside to this approach," his accountant warned, "someday you'll sell. The tax bill when that happens—it could be really high." To ensure he wouldn't have an un-payable tax bill, Larry knew he needed a larger future cashflow.

To do that, he would have to make something out of

nothing. While serving on the City Planning Commission, Larry noticed developers coming in to request zoning changes. Residential to commercial, and from single-family to multi-family. The latter was the one that had Larry's interest since he had two houses near Southern Oregon College. When he checked the zoning, he saw that both lots were already multi-family.

All he had to do was replace the houses with apartments. For that he would need money and contacts who knew how to build new construction.

To get the money, Larry knew he needed to increase his income. His consulting engineering business wasn't going much better than the first time he had been self-employed. After sending out letters and talking to people in his various service clubs, he learned that Marquess and Associates had lost their Electrical Engineer. He contacted Walt Marquess and soon began the interview process, culminating with an offer:

"I'll take you on as an employee," Walt said.

Larry, however, didn't want to be an employee again. He knew that it was time for him to take control of his own destiny. He said, "I'm sticking to my guns. I'll be an independent consultant or we can partner up."

"Roner's been doing mechanical engineering and Westwood's been doing civil engineering. I don't want them to lose their invested equity. I can do a partnership between you and me for Electrical Engineering. You'll have an office in the Goldy Building and a salary of twelve dollars an hour. With my Structural Engineering, we can offer four vital services under one roof."

Larry thought about it for approximately two heartbeats. "Deal."

His full time partnership with Marquess required him to merge his electrical engineering contracts with the new business. When he worked long into the night at home, it was for this new partnership. In addition to his electrical engineering work, Larry became the corporate secretary, taking notes on all of the things the company planned and did through the years.

The first year of business with Marquess was slow. However, it did lead Larry to a critical investment opportunity. While collaborating on designing electrical systems for Southern Oregon College's Music Building, Larry met the lead architect, Vince Oredson.

They carpooled together on a trip to Eugene. As they took the sweeping interstate curves through the Siskiyou Mountains, they started talking. Larry sensed that an architect would be one of the professional contacts he needed to convert his lots in Ashland. "I've got two lots next to Southern College, multi-family."

"No kidding?" Vince asked.

"What I haven't figured out yet, is what to do with them."

"I might be able to help with that. Me and this other guy, we just developed a set of apartments in Ashland— Takilma Village. We got a HUD loan on it. Almost nothing down. Problem is, he wants to sell, and I want to do another one."

"What's he asking?"

"Ten grand. Why don't you buy his half? You've already got the two lots. We can take those and build another thirty two units. Between the two of them we'll each own fifty-percent of fifty units."

"Why's he so hot to sell?" Larry asked.

"They're HUD funded. That limits how much annual return we can take out, what kind of management fees we can charge, all that. Right now we're getting a little more than five percent return. The advantage of going HUD is the government will do one-hundred percent financing—we don't have to put anything down."

When Larry looked over the project's books, he saw that between allowable rental income and tax breaks for depreciation he would make an annual 10% return on investment. He explained it to Ann with the simple: "What a deal."

Larry and Vince formed a partnership called Ashland Better Housing. They began work on the new apartments. Larry was able to give all the engineering work to Marquess and Associates.

His engineering firm wasn't the only beneficiary of added work. Chuck had recently helped Larry install electricity at the Diamond Lake cabin. Larry had been impressed with Chuck's aptitude for construction work. Over dinner, Larry mentioned, "Merle Howard is looking for able bodies to help with construction of the new apartments." Chuck took the job. He quickly learned the basics of construction and was able to take on as much work as he could handle.

A few weeks in, Larry and Ann were awoken by a call in the night: Chuck had been in an accident. Ann and Larry scrambled to the car and drove to the scene where their pickup truck was totaled against a tree.

"What happened?" Larry couldn't decide where to look: the crumpled hood of the truck, the bloody rag Chuck held to his nose, or the tree that stood stalwart in the night. He checked the street and lawn the truck had crossed but saw no skid marks.

"I missed my turn," Chuck said.

"How'd you do that?" Larry asked.

"I think I fell asleep." Chuck had been putting in double shifts at the new apartment buildings, sacrificing sleep so that he could earn more money. Larry cringed as he'd habitually sacrificed sleep for income, but with the benefit of a home office—no driving tired.

"Let's see your nose," Ann said.

Chuck pulled the bloody rag away.

"That looks smashed," Ann said.

"The steering wheel woke me up." Chuck tried to laugh.

"I'm just glad you're okay," Ann said. But her feelings went deeper than that. Chuck Sr. had died when he wasn't much older than Chuck was now. If his last earthy legacy had died—no, more than that, he wasn't just Chuck Sr.'s legacy, he was her son, and the love of a mother overwhelmed her in that moment. He was her son, and she nearly lost him that night.

17

If it is to be...
Medford 1971

In early 1971, Larry and Vince had the ribbon cutting ceremony for their newly-named Chief Tyee Apartments. The first ten units were officially open for rent. The sound of construction and the mingling smells of fresh sawdust and asphalt backdropped the ceremony. The remaining units would be completed later that year.

Larry didn't have to look far to find his first managers—his recently retired father and mother moved from Portland to oversee the property.

Larry was thrilled to finally have another reliable income stream that would provide for his oncoming retirement. Travel between Medford and Ashland became faster with the recently completed Interstate 5. However, he had an idea, which he shared with Ann, "What about Medford? We could build more here," Larry said.

"Does Vince have an idea for another complex?"

Larry shook his head. "Why have a partner if you can do everything yourself? If it is to be, it is up to me." Larry grinned. First, he needed a site for the project. He found an acre of undeveloped land off Spring Street. His next challenge was to convince the city to approve the project. It would prove to be a non-challenge, as unknown to Larry, the Medford City Council had recently voted to expand low-cost housing.

The hard part was getting approval from the bank for a construction loan. Larry met with a loan broker. The bank's conference room had poor lighting and uncomfortable chairs. The banker narrowed his brows. "How big a project is the—what are they called?"

"Julia Ann. Named for my wife," Larry said.

"That's sweet. How many units?"

"I want to do seventy-two units," Larry said.

The broker crossed his arms. "That's way too many. We'll never get that approved."

"We have the five-plex, the eight-plex, the units in Ashland—"

"You can't use those. HUD won't let you use their units as collateral." The broker tapped a pen on the table and shook his head. "You've got too many liabilities. A house on Highland? Another in Ashland? Your primary residence? I don't see how it'll work."

"We can take our equity out of the house on Highland. Dump the house and free up that liability. There's Ann's wealth in the store."

The broker continued to shake his head.

Larry mulled on this a moment. "Can we do fifty-six?"

The broker's head-shake finally changed to a nod. "Yeah. I think I can get that approved."

The construction loan went through.

The fifty-six units comprising the Julia Ann apartments were built. Once construction completed, a long-term HUD issued loan was applied to the property. Larry's total investment was $30,000. Several years later, Juila Ann, Chief Tyee, and Takilma Villiage were refinanced at a value of $2.5 Million dollars.

As part of the deal, they took all of Ann's equity out of the Highland house and gifted the mortgaged property to Chuck, a move fundamentally similar to mortgaging a property in Monopoly before handing it to another player —they gifted ownership. Ownership being key to unlocking opportunity.

At home, Ann and Larry were celebrating the opening of Julia Ann apartments when a story came on the news.

"During maneuvers off Hon La Island in North Vietnam, the USS Bausell came under fire by enemy forces on the shore…" the newscaster informed.

"The Bausell. That's Craig's ship, isn't it?" Ann asked.

Larry turned up the television volume.

"…The ship was participating in fire-support when it was struck by a single shell…"

Larry's hands tightened on the arms of his chair. He didn't realize he had stopped breathing. He willed the newscaster to speak faster and more to the point.

"…Resulting in a small onboard fire. There are no confirmed US casualties at this time."

It had been years since Larry attended church, but in this moment he said a silent and heartfelt prayer for his son's safety.

Several months later, he received a letter from Craig that included the photo of a woman he intended to marry. His son had both survived the battle at sea and found the love of his life. There was a small catch. Craig's fiance, Jane Hidalgo was a foreign national from the Philippines and the Navy had yet to approve the marriage. Larry wanted to help Craig, so he approached John Dellenback, former congressman for Southern Oregon. The picture and the letter were enough to get the congressman on the matter. Approvals went through in less than two weeks. A wedding invitation followed.

Hot on the heels of the joyous letter, was a letter from Larry's partner in Ashland, Vince Oredson offering to sell his half of the partnership.

Larry was livid. The price was too high. "Almost double its value," Larry muttered.

Needing a strategy, Larry poured over the contract they had signed, looking for a way to force a fair market buyout. What he found, was a peculiar bit of wording that described how one partner could offer to sell to the other, and if they didn't buy at that rate, turn around and buy the other one's share.

"I can retaliate on price," Larry told Ann.

"Retaliate?"

"He started the price war. He doesn't have any money —I might as well buy him for under market," Larry said. He sent Vince a letter offering to sell at below market prices, knowing Vince had no money for the purchase. When Vince didn't respond, Larry invoked the contract's clause to force a sale at the price Larry wanted to pay.

Vince's response made Larry pale.

"What's wrong?" Ann asked.

"Oh boy," Larry said. "He got a lawyer."

During negotiations, Vince argued that he was never paid for architectural work on Chief Tyee, thus the inflated buyout price.

At home, Larry kept Ann up to date on the developments, saying, "If he wanted to be paid, he should have put it in the contract!"

"You do contract work," Ann said. "You like to be paid."

"I ask for it in the contract. If I don't ask to be paid, I don't go and ask for it later. I donated time to the project."

"And if you were selling, you'd want to be reimbursed for that time, wouldn't you?" Ann asked.

"Well. I'm not selling."

Ann countered: "My grandfather used to have a saying. Always do the right thing."

Larry threw his hands up in exasperation. Ann was right. Vince had not been paid for his time and skills. Larry too had donated time to the project, but since Vince was exiting the partnership, Larry could appreciate Vince's desire to zero the bookkeeping. They reached a settlement for fair market value plus Vince's professional work.

Larry found himself the sole owner of both Ashland Better Housing, and Medford Better Housing.

18

A Wedding Abroad
Manila Philipines 1973

Larry and Ann's second international trip took them to Manila, Philippines, for the wedding of his oldest son, Craig. Roughly one and a half million people were squeezed into just over forty square kilometers, making the city roughly twice as dense as New York.

Before Craig's wedding, Larry and Ann were able to meet Jane and Jane's boss for lunch. Philippine traditions expected bosses to be more personal than in the United States, thus the inclusion of Jane's boss for the first meeting between Jane and her fiancé's parents.

"How'd you end up in the Philippines?" Larry asked Craig.

"It started when I met Jane's brother at Navy fire-fighting school," Craig said. "He gave me her name, and I started writing her letters. I thought, 'how am I going to get to the Philippines?' The Navy was sending a bunch of ships to Osaka. My PT one-hundred crew helped me transfer to the USS Bausell. From Osaka, I caught a plane to the Navy base here in the Philippines. I called on her at work."

"I was surprised," Jane said. She spoke English with only a slight accent. "I had been going to church every day and praying to St. Jude—our patron saint—to bring me a husband. I knew the first time I met Craig that he was the one."

"Mom, Dad, I really appreciate you came over for my wedding. You didn't have to do that," Craig said.

"It is our pleasure," Larry said.

"It's a huge expense, both time and money," Craig said.

"No expense at all." Larry spread his hands, palms down to dismiss any notion that this had put him out. While Craig was right, it was a huge expense of time and money, Larry was never one to let anyone in the family feel like they had put strain on either of those resources. But the truth of it went like this: "You could have chosen anywhere in the world to get married, and we would go." It was a tradition that Larry and Ann upheld for all of their children and grandchildren.

It was a full-church wedding with the entire congregation in attendance, starting with Mass before moving to the marriage rights. The three Hortons were the only Americans in attendance. The ceremony began with the bride giving coins to the groom and an exchange of rings. Craig and Jane placed veils over each other's heads before they lit candles. The ends of a cord were placed around each other's necks as they exchanged vows.

A reception followed the wedding, where Ann and Larry were able to sample more Philippine cuisine. The nation's history as a colony of China, then Spain, the United States, and even Japan led to a melting pot of flavors. Most dishes carry an unlikely combination of sweet, sour, and salty. Of course, there was beef adobo with its seasoning of crushed garlic, bay leaves, peppercorns, and soy sauce with a vinegar base. Barbecued chicken, mountains of rice, and fried fish were just a few other dishes. But the main course dominated all of the others: Lechon, a spit roasted pig with crisp golden-brown skin served with liver sauce.

During the reception, Larry and Ann were able to meet Jane's mother, who told them, "It's always been a dream of mine for one of my children to have a full-church wedding."

19

Golden Age of the Hortons
Southern Oregon 1973

Home from the adventures in the Philippines, Larry resumed work on a recently started project: Northwood. Several years back Larry had wandered the soon-to-be site of the Julia Ann apartments. At the time the lot had been a mixture of clay soil and hardpan. He walked around the site, visualizing where the apartments and parking spaces would eventually go. It was then that the owner of an adjacent property approached him.

"I've got two acres. Two old houses. I'm renting one at forty a month. The other is empty. Maybe the land would be a boon to your project," the property owner said.

"What are your price and terms?" Larry asked.

"If you can pay fifteen thousand over seven years at seven percent we have a deal."

"What do you need down?"

"Ten dollars would do."

They shook hands on the spot. Larry acquired an adjacent half-acre and found himself in possession of a huge stretch of real estate that was already on path to becoming Northwood Apartments, and would soon grow past that. The State of Oregon had instituted a program for Section 8 housing for the elderly. This would prove to be Larry's most ambitious deal to date. As he described it to Ann, "The construction cost for thirty-six units is estimated at five-hundred and twenty-thousand dollars. Half of those are two bedrooms. The land has a value of fifty-four thousand..." Larry was so excited to explain the deal to Ann that it wasn't until he was near the end that he noticed she was just smiling and nodding. Still, he continued explaining the deal, part for her sake, and part to make sure he had full understanding of it, "...access is from Crater Lake Avenue through a thirty-by-four-hundred foot drive—we can upgrade that later when we get Northwood Avenue put through—then we finally can get approved for the State of Oregon Bond Loan."

Ann was still just smiling and nodding. It was the reaction this deal got from everyone Larry had presented it to.

"If anything happens to me on this trip to Minnesota, just forget about the project. It's so complicated that nobody else can figure it out," Larry said.

Amidst the excitement of preparing for Northwood, Larry received additional exciting news: Craig had a son. Larry's first grandchild was born at the US Naval hospital in Osaka. Three months later, Craig was discharged from the Navy. He, his wife, and infant son returned to the Rogue Valley. Larry continued the tradition of providing employment to family and friends, giving both Craig and Jane positions within the rapidly growing Medford Better Housing.

Northwood turned out to be a very lucrative deal. Larry had to put up $150,000 in capital, with the bank covering the rest. To gain enough money for the project, he refinanced and sold his eight-plex to Craig and sold all his remaining stocks. When Northwood was complete, Larry's parents, Gene and Retta moved in as property managers. They had previously managed both Chief Tyee and Julia Ann apartments.

After Northwood, Larry turned his attention on another project, Eastwood. The State of Oregon was looking for a sponsor for a twenty-four unit property. Northwood had depleted all of Larry's on hand cash and credit. He looked for partners on this deal. Luckily, he didn't have to look farther than Marquess and Associates. Each of the engineers put up money for the project. All they needed was land. Larry soon found a reasonable site. It was three acres, just under $60,000, and zoned for multi-family.

Larry walked the site, something he had taken to doing since the Julia Ann apartments. As he visualized where the buildings and parking would go, he realized: "Twenty-four units aren't going to fill the land. There's space for forty units here." A revelation he presented to the Oregon State department of Housing and Urban Development.

The State Housing Director met with Larry at his office: "There are already too many low-income houses in that area. Julia Ann, Northwood, Springdale Terrace, the Spring St Apartments, Hawthorne Gardens, and the elderly living community on Royal."

"The extra sixteen will have no additional impact," Larry said. "They will simply be part of the twenty four."

The Director shook his head. "The area is already saturated. We want twenty four in Medford, not in this neighborhood."

Larry had already bought the land and had faith that there was demand for the units. His campaign to get the approval included calls to the local congressman and a letter-writing campaign to the state. The project was approved.

The State Housing Director met with Larry again. "You shouldn't be doing that."

"Doing what?"

"Trying to strong arm the State. We asked for a sponsor for twenty-four units, not forty," the Director said.

"We had land for forty."

"I don't care what you do with your land. The state wanted twenty-four units. You shouldn't put undue influence on Government. We're trying to help the people, not businessmen."

Unfazed by the rebuke, Larry continued to pursue opportunities. News of the income he was generating from his rental developments spread, and soon he was approached by Ed Clay, whose office was adjacent to Larry's in the Goldy building.

"I rent pasture from Charles Gore," Ed said.

"Pasture?" Larry prodded.

"For my horses. But that isn't the point. This pasture, it's close to town. It's a good-sized lot. You could do another one of your apartments there," Ed said.

"Is he interested in selling?" Larry asked.

"He's interested in a partnership," Ed said.

Larry went to work on evaluating the value of Gore's land. He reached a fair market value of $50,000. Gore would put up the land; Ed and Larry would match the value with cash. This was initially planned to follow the same program they used to make the Julia Ann low-income, family housing. The community protested. To get the development approved, they had to shift to low-income senior housing, taking advantage of the same section 8 for the elderly that Larry had utilized with Northwood.

Larry wanted thirty-six units on the land. For that, he needed an appraisal in excess of five million or the bank wouldn't loan the money to develop. The first appraisal came back low. Larry tore it up and threw it away.

He knew the value was there. He decided to get as many appraisals as it took to find someone who shared Larry's vision for the property.

When Larry finally received an appraisal that was high enough for the loan, he moved forward. The last thing standing in the way of the project was a zoning change. At the preliminary city council meeting, several local residents stood to speak. They complained that the low-income housing would bring noise, traffic, and crime to an otherwise peaceful neighborhood.

Among the opposition was Jim Dunphy, the closest neighbor to the project. "This is a quiet neighborhood. I didn't buy this house so I could have a loud apartment behind it."

As the city council vote neared, Larry met with anyone on the council that would take his appointment, including Council Member Hugh Jennings.

"Look, the city is getting in the way of what I want to do with my land," Larry said.

"It's your land," Jennings said, "but it's zoned single family."

"There's a real need for low-income housing right now," Larry said. "Just last month city council voted to demolish the Linger Longer Mobile Park just down the street. Where are those people going to live?"

"You have me there. I could agree to an amended proposal. One with strictly limited occupancy to replace the displaced housing from the mobile park," Jennings said.

Even with Hugh's vote, Larry didn't have enough support to get the change approved. He met with Attorney Frank VanDyke in an attempt to find a legal solution to force council support.

"The outspoken neighbor, Dunphy, he works with councilman Bill Tycer at Pacific Power. They're both IBEW union members. Jim must be influencing Bill."

"If Bill has a conflict of interest, he's got to announce it," Frank said.

"Bill stopped returning my calls," Larry said.

"You said they both work at the power company," Frank said, "you could check with their manager. Maybe explain to him that Bill needs to declare his conflict of interest."

Larry visited Bill Parrett, the Medford manager for Pacific Power and Light where both Tycer and Dunphy were employed.

"I've been trying to get through to Bill Tycer," Larry said.

"Sure, I know Bill. A good guy. He's on city council," Parrett said.

"The problem is, he works with the neighbor to this project. I think he has a conflict of interest," Larry said.

"I'm really not sure what you want me to do," Parrett said.

"Since he won't talk to me. If you could get him to listen. Well, I think there are three options." Larry held up one finger. "He could stay home from the meeting entirely." Larry held up a second finger. "He could change his vote to support the application." Larry held up a third finger. "Abstain from voting."

"What if he doesn't want to do one of those?" Parrett said.

"I'd be forced to file suit against the city and Tycer claiming the councilman had engaged in *ex parte* contacts with an opponent of the project. And I'll drop my past vocal opposition to the public utility district movement which is trying to edge PP&L out of Jackson County," Larry said.

The city council vote was tied, half for and half against the rezoning. The mayor, Al Densmore broke the tie by voting in favor of the rezoning. Councilman Tycer only had icy glares for Larry.

After the vote, Larry got a call from David Force with the Mail Tribune. "Is it true you put pressure on Bill Tycer?"

Larry, out of habit, answered with full honesty, "I did put some pressure on him. No question about it. We warned him ahead of time what was coming if he didn't change his vote. This world is made up of pressures."

A story ran a few days later in the Mail Tribune under the headline: "Developer Admits Pressure on Council." Among other things Larry learned from the story, was that Bill Tycer had gone to the city attorney to bring suit against Larry. The attorney had felt the case was too shaky and relied too heavily on hearsay. Larry had been on the cusp of a major lawsuit.

Larry was devastated.

Ann attempted to console him. "I'm sure it will pass."

"I always try to do the right thing and be honest with my dealings." Larry scratched at his arms. The nervousness was making him itch.

The fallout from the story's publication was rapid and severe. The County Commission asked Larry to resign from the Housing Authority of Jackson County, where he had previously had a six year membership, including chairing over the change of executive officers. Worse still, the mayor called Larry.

"I need you to resign from the Architectural Review Commission," Al said.

"Why?"

"It's an election year. If I don't do something to punish you for putting pressure on the council, then someone might run a story implicating you put pressure on me as well," Al said.

"That would be a lie," Larry said.

"Look, I don't know how accurate that story in the Tribune was. What I do know is I can't afford bad press right now. You got your project approved. Now you're going to have to resign."

For most of the next year, Larry was afraid everyone in town would cut ties with him over the pressures he had exerted over council.

Work on the T'Morrow for the Elderly apartments was completed in 1980. Ed Clay died a few months later. Larry gave his widow a favorable buyout. Soon after that, Gorr began to experience medical problems. Every few years he sold another chunk of ownership to Larry until finally, Larry was the sole owner of the T'Morrow for the Elderly Apartments.

20

Murder at Diamond Lake
Medford 1974

On August 8th, Richard Nixon resigned his position as President of the United States to avoid a vote for his Impeachment as result of the tapes leaked in the Watergate scandal. Ann, a lifelong Republican was still feeling the effects from the historic resignation two weeks later when her model 500 telephone rang in the kitchen.

When she answered, the voice on the other end of the line was frantic: "Have you heard from Mom?"

Adrenaline hit Ann. Heard from Mom? "Bob? What's…Mom is at Diamond Lake with Dad—"

But her brother Bob cut her off with, "The State Police called—Dad's dead."

Ann felt the air pulled from her lungs. Dad's…she barely muttered, "Dead?" There was a ringing in her ears.

"I'm going to Mom's." Bob's voice sounded tinny and distant. Ann was having difficulty focusing.

"I'll meet you there," she without realizing she spoke. Her hand shook as she placed the receiver in the cradle. Chuck Sr. had died, her son Chuck had nearly died from an auto accident, and now her father…dead.

She was in a daze as she stumbled from the kitchen.

"Something wrong?" Larry asked as he stepped out of his home office.

"Arnel's dead."

"What? How?" Larry dropped the sheaf of papers from his face, but Ann was seeing through the tunnel of shock and had trouble making out his features.

"I don't know," Ann managed. "I have to go to Mom's."

"I'll drive you," Larry said.

It was a silent, tense drive the few short blocks from their house to Elsie's house. Even in late August, Ann felt a chill as she got out of the car and walked along the sidewalk she had played on as a child.

Bob paced in front of the house.

"Where's Mom?" Ann asked.

Bob shook his head. "I don't know. I don't know."

The late afternoon heat baked Ann. When she heard the pitter of a Volkswagen Bug engine, she looked up with earnestness. Elsie's canary yellow car pulled into the driveway.

"What a surprise to see you all," Elsie said.

"Mom, did you hear?" Ann blurted.

"Hear what?"

"Dad's dead," Bob said.

Elsie's face paled. Bob and Ann ran to her, but Elsie shook her head once in a resolute no. They retired inside for ice water.

"I always worry about him, up there all alone," Elsie said. She sipped her water. "In the mountains. By himself." She dabbed at the corners of her eyes with a kerchief.

Her phone rang. Bob and Ann looked at the phone, silently deciding who would answer, when Elsie walked past them. "I'll get it." She answered and listened. An occasional, "Yes…that's me…I understand…yes…Bruno…okay…yes…we'll send someone."

Elsie cradled the receiver. She didn't wilt, but instead looked distant, vacant, but somehow resolute. Finally, something changed in her and she looked at Ann and Bob and smiled. The pain bled through the edges of her smile.

"Bruno…" that was their dog. Elsie kept reddening eyes open as she repeated, "He was guarding Arnel's body. It took the police half an hour to calm him."

Ann and Bob rushed to Elsie's side. "They need someone to go to Roseburg, to identify the body," Elsie said.

"I'll go," Bob volunteered.

"I can go," Ann said.

Bob shook his head. "Stay with Mom."

"I need to get a change of clothes for him," Elsie said. When neither Ann nor Bob said anything, Elsie added, "They found him in his swimming suit at the dinner table. The back of his head was smashed in."

Ann and Bob exchanged stunned looks. Elsie went through the glass doors to the back bedrooms…the same glass doors that Ann had broken when Bob had locked her into their parents's room when she was a young girl. The terror of that moment wrapped itself around the shock she was feeling—making her body shake.

Elsie came back with one of Arnel's suits. Her hands trembled as she handed the suit to Bob. "They have a suspect—his killer—I'm not sure. A boy. I met him."

"You met him?" Bob asked.

"A hitch-hiker—a runaway. He stole Arnel's car." Arnel had a Volkswagen Transporter Type 2, commonly known as the Microbus, or simply a VW Bus. Elsie shook her head. Ann had never seen her unflappable mother out of sorts like this. "He was camping nearby. After I left...he must have...it's all my fault. I shouldn't have left him alone."

Ann held her mother and said, "It's not your fault."

Bob left with a change of clothes for his father—and to identify the body. The next few days were full of confusion and grief. Larry drove north to meet with the attorney who represented the family at the trial. He shared what he learned with Ann.

"The kid was a runaway. Arnel invited him over for dinner, and the kid, he bashed Arnel over the head with a frying pan and took the car. Just drove off. But he didn't know how to work the dimmers. So he stopped at a ranger station. The ranger recognized the plates: ARNEL."

"What's going to happen to the boy?" Ann asked.

"He's a minor," Larry said. "So they're giving him probation and banishing him from Southern Oregon."

"He murdered my father." Ann's voice broke. "And that's it? Probation? That's not justice."

"I know." Larry held Ann in a tight hug.

Because of the wounds suffered, Arnel's body was cremated in Roseburg. The family held a memorial service for him at St. Mark's Episcopal Church in Medford.

21

Passing the Torch
Medford 1974

The living room floor vibrated up and down by noise that resolved over time into music. Jerry and his band were practicing downstairs again. Larry sipped his coffee and flipped through the mail. One letter was from his son, Stan, who had graduated with a degree in Journalism from the University of Oregon, and now had his first job with the Honolulu Star-Advertiser.

Larry looked closer at the envelope. "Ann, do you recognize this stamp?"

"What?" She had to yell over the music coming from downstairs.

Larry pointed at the stamp.

"Isn't that one of those new issues we sent Stan?" Ann yelled.

"I thought he was collecting them!" Larry sighed. Stan had been an avid stamp collector in his youth, and Larry had been sending him plate blocks of new issues. It looked like Stan's time of collecting stamps, however, had come to an end. Larry smiled to himself. It seemed like just yesterday that his boys had been competing for the last piece of roast or asking for help with their homework.

Larry and Ann had been planning to visit Stan in Hawaii. However, as Larry learned in the letter, Stan had taken a job with the Oregonian in Portland as the Editor of the *TV Click*.

That summer, over Fourth of July weekend, Larry and Ann attended the wedding of Chuck and Sue Bratton. Chuck and Sue met at Oregon State University where they both graduated with degrees in Teaching. They spent one year teaching at Taft, in Lincoln City, Oregon, before returning to Medford where Chuck returned to carpentry. He worked on Larry's newest project, Johnston Manor, before earning his contractor's license and building his own home in Medford.

One of the projects he undertook was a remodel of Lawrence's Jewelers, which recently moved to its final location in downtown Medford. Ann and her brother, Bob, continued to work at the jewelry store. Ann's mother, Elsie, now retired from teaching, donated her time to the store. Another member of the family worked at the store as well: Jerry.

He asked Chuck, "They got you working here too?"

"Just remodeling, so there will be more room for china," Chuck said. "How's the engraving going?"

"It's going. I'm finishing up a jewelry repair course out at Southern Oregon College," Jerry said. "We won't have to contract out as much jewelry repair."

"Why don't you keep working here?" Ann asked Chuck.

"It would be a pay-cut, but it would be consistent income," Chuck said. The consistent income was especially important because he and Sue were starting a family and there weren't any construction jobs in January.

He demonstrated a hard work ethic and business aptitude.

While Jerry was making money at the store, his passion was rock and roll. He moved his full drum set out of his parent's basement when he married Judy Henderson in 1975. The two of them lived in the house that Larry had moved from the site of Northwood along with Judy's son from a previous marriage. Jerry worked to support his family and his band. He went on to perform concerts throughout Southern Oregon and Northern California.

Jerry wasn't the only son with an interest in music and the arts. Steve had spent his first summer out of high school in Ashland, helping out wherever he could with the Oregon Shakespeare Festival. He had the theater bug, performing in among others, the Community Players Group of West Lynn as an avid semi-professional. While attempting to break into the Portland theater scene, he met and later married Sue Spinnet in 1978.

"How's the job hunt going?" Larry asked Steve.

"Not well. I need to get something. Sue's pregnant. We're going to have another mouth to feed," Steve said.

Larry thought he had the perfect solution: "We're looking for a manager at Chief Tyee. It's near the Shakespeare Festival. You'll have a house and income for incidentals."

Steve took him up on the offer.

Four of the sons were now married, living in the Rogue Valley, and starting families of their own. This gave Ann and Larry plenty of excuses to spoil their many grandchildren—sometimes Ann even returned from the Los Angeles gift show with toys that wouldn't be released for months, giving her grandchildren early access to some of the season's hottest products.

Craig and Steve both managed property for Larry, while Chuck and Jerry worked at the family Jewelry store with Ann. The only son still out of the area was Stan, who got engaged to Nancy Kirsch. Nancy had waitressed at a diner that Stan frequented before she went on to graduate from Clark College and become a Registered Nurse. They were married in Camas, Washington, in 1980. All five of Larry and Ann's boys had matching Tuxedos for the event. Stan never moved back to Medford.

The rampant inflation of the 1970's had been a source of worry for Larry. He talked to Ann about it: "There is a question in my mind as to how we can plan for retirement when prices are going up this fast. I didn't do well at the commodities market...I'm not sure how we can take advantage of the situation to grow our investments."

"Is there a book you can read on it?" Ann asked.

"I've read all the books on the subject. None of them deal with times of great inflation," Larry said.

"All the books?" Ann laughed. Larry's voracious appetite for self-help books was another symptom of his work ethic. "There has to be someone in the valley who knows how to invest in this market," Ann said.

A thought began to form in Larry's mind. "You're right. I've met all number of successful businessmen through Kiwanis and City Government. Why should I be the only one who learns? Four of our boys are here."

"What are you planning?" Ann asked.

"Breakfasts. Every Saturday morning. I can make pancakes," Larry said. "We can keep a log book and write-up minutes of the meetings." Larry's participation in social clubs had made him a strong believer in parliamentary procedure and record keeping. More important than that, however, he felt these meetings with business leaders would help his boys get a leg up on the competition—and possibly help them avoid the trouble Larry had run into with the city council.

Only the four local boys attended the breakfasts, but occasionally Stan would drive down from Portland to visit. This time, it was because of Stan's upcoming birthday.

"Every birthday I miss Mom," Stan said. "That spice cake she would always make for me." Stan both shook and nodded his head at the same time. "I've never been able to get Nancy to quite duplicate it."

"What is really weird," Craig started, "the guy, Dr. Mario Campagna...the one who operated on mother. Jane and I, we go to church and I see him there all the time. Last week, I went to talk to him and I thanked him for trying to save mother's life. It's just odd that I see him every week in church."

"I wish I could have repaid her for saving my life," Steve said. "What an angel." The boys's rare moment of shared emotion was cut short by a knock at the door.

Over the next months, guest speakers came to the meetings: Harold Ellis with State Farm; Barney Baxter who dealt with investing; Jerry Laytham, operations manager at the Mail Tribune; Virginia Vogel, CPA; Mike Neyt, an Executive with Bank of Southern Oregon; Doctor Carrol Elgin, who was able to retire early off investments; and local businessmen like Jerry Baird and Wally Iverson.

"Dad, these Saturday meetings, they're pretty cool," Craig said.

"Are you learning from them?" Larry asked.

"It's interesting how much leaders read," Craig said.

"I'm anxious to try some of this investing out," Chuck said.

Larry reflected on this idea. He'd been raised in poverty, and had to hustle for every opportunity he had. He wondered if he could help his boys to a faster start. "Let's create a Horton Family Partnership. I can supply the initial capital. We can all share in the profits."

Everyone was in agreement to try.

"What should we invest in first?" Larry asked.

"What about gold?" Jerry offered. "I've been studying about it in school. It's reached some pretty high values."

"Let's plot its course on paper first," Larry said, "because I think the value is going to fall." It did, but they hadn't learned enough about the market yet to take advantage of the decline in value.

Watching gold fall created an ah-ha moment for Chuck. "Commodities are amazing. It's like what we've been learning from the speakers—use a small amount of capital to control large profits. Being able to control five-thousand worth of gold for only a five-hundred dollar margin!"

Instead of instantly crushing Chuck's optimism with the story of his own substantial losses in commodities, Larry said, "Why don't you make some trades on paper and see how it works out?"

A month later, Chuck returned with a hand-written ledger. "Forty profitable trades in a row." He laid the paper in front of Larry.

Larry was suitably impressed. "I'll setup an account so you can trade for the trust."

A few weeks later, Chuck returned with a beaming grin on his face.

"How's the trading going?" Larry asked.

"Twenty profitable trades. I might be able to quit working and just do this," Chuck said.

"Oh?"

"Look at this." Chuck took a quick breath and began to explain things in rapid fashion, "They still haven't sold last year's crop of cocoa! And they have a bumper crop this year! The price has to go down!"

"Chuck, the price doesn't have to go down," Larry said.

"Yes, it does!" Chuck was highly animated.

"Well, sell it. But the price doesn't have to go down. There are people who use their own money to manipulate the markets, to keep the prices from going up or down."

Chuck frowned. "That's not how the market works. It self corrects. It's all about supply and demand."

Larry didn't react. He knew Chuck was a devout believer in the market's ability to self-regulate. At the same time, he knew there were other forces at work. But deep down, a part of Larry wanted Chuck to prove him wrong and succeed in commodities where he had failed. If Chuck really had the secret of the markets, Larry's desire for mastery wanted to know.

The next day, Chuck checked back in with Larry.

"I've sold short. Cocoa's going down. I think I can pyramid this. Start small and make a fortune on one trade. This is the one I can do it on. I'm using my profits from the first trade to sell two more contracts. This could make a million dollars."

Larry sat at his desk and thought about the possibility of this. It betrayed everything that was Larry's personal investing philosophy. Larry did not believe in getting rich quick. His process was much more methodical: find something that works and repeat it indefinitely. He preferred the slow, true burn. What Chuck proposed sounded more like a flash-fire. Still, Larry said nothing. He had placed Chuck in charge of the trading account and was willing to wait and see if Chuck was indeed right.

A few days later, Chuck returned. "Cocoa isn't moving as fast as I thought it should—if it's this obvious to me it should be to everyone."

"Things are complicated like that," Larry said.

"I put in stops, so we won't lose money," Chuck said.

Larry nodded. He refused to interfere. However, Larry had been checking cocoa futures constantly since Chuck had first shown interest.

The next afternoon, Chuck returned. "It started up."

"It started up," Larry echoed. He'd already seen the morning report.

"Took out all my stops. Then…fell right off the table." Chuck dropped his hand away dramatically. "If I hadn't put in those stops, we might have made a hundred-thousand today."

"What's the next deal going to be?" Larry asked.

Chuck chewed on his fingernails. Larry wasn't sure, but it looked like they were bleeding.

"You were right again," Chuck said. "I'm not sure I'm fit to do this. I'm starting to get heartburn."

Larry could commiserate. His own ventures into commodities had gone considerably worse. But Larry had been trading with his own money—money he knew he could replace, and Larry realized that trading with someone else's money had only compounded the strain on Chuck.

Larry had wished in this instance that he had been wrong. Chuck had seemed on the cusp of market mastery.

It was a thing nearly everyone in the family attempted at one point in their lives. While Chuck wasn't able to make a hundred-thousand dollar trade, his investing acumen was good enough to double their initial capital from $2500 to $5000 in a short period of time.

At the next breakfast, Larry brought up a new opportunity, "I heard about a restaurant in Coburg that needs some capital."

Chuck and Larry drove up the freeway to investigate. It was a combination restaurant and bar. The manager showed them around. "We're making decent money at the bar but our food sales aren't as good as we'd like. The food's good, we just want to make the restaurant a little more family friendly. That's where the money comes in. Some decorations, a new sign, that sort of thing."

Chuck and Larry tried several of the restaurant's dishes.

"What do you think?" Larry asked.

"The food seems okay." Chuck shrugged. "It looks a little empty in here." Chuck and Larry had the restaurant to themselves.

"Once we finish remodeling, this place is going to be just as packed as the bar," the manager said. "You'll get your money back in no-time."

They agreed to invest $10,000 in the restaurant. Six months later, Larry had bad news for the boys, "The restaurant in Coburg filed for bankruptcy today."

"Do we get anything back?" Steve asked.

Larry shook his head. "The investment's gone."

"What happened?" Craig asked.

The restaurant's facelift failed to increase clientele. Apparently it wasn't the look of the place that scared families away, but the rowdy bar full of drunks. The restaurant continued to make more food than could be sold, with hundreds of dollars worth of food spoiling each night.

Larry was disappointed by the loss of money, but, with his usual positive thinking, found a way to spin the situation. "Let's think of this as a learning experience. What can we take away from this?"

"There's a reason why people need money," Chuck said.

Larry nodded.

"We didn't ask enough questions up front," Craig said.

Larry nodded again.

"None of us knew about restaurants," Jerry said.

Another nod from Larry.

"Don't keep feeding a loser," Steve said.

Larry slapped the table. "That's right. Take your losses and go onto something else."

Their next investment opportunity came from outside the Saturday meeting group. Larry explained it to Ann over a dinner of sloppy joes and pasta salad: "Our investment group had its first big success today. Jane's house closed." Craig's wife, Jane, had found a local seller —a rarity since the housing market's recent collapse.

"Did the boys negotiate a good deal?" Ann asked.

"Forty-three thousand with payments of eight hundred and fifty dollars a month," Larry said. "They'll have the house paid off in no-time."

"That was fortuitous Jane found the seller," Ann said.

"It really was. In this market…it's hard to find a house for sale. The boys are giving her a five percent finder's fee," Larry said.

"All these breakfasts are paying off," Ann said.

"They really are. They showed me something else, too. All this real-estate we've been acquiring, it's going to take care of our retirement with no difficulty," Larry said.

22

On to A Class
Rogue Valley 1978

Blue Air's fourth place Northwest Regional finish earned Ann and Larry local celebrity. The Rogue Valley Yacht Club promoted Larry to Western Vice Commodore and the club urged Larry and Ann to race in the All-Sails class.

"That means the spinnaker," Ann said. It was an oversized, brightly colored sail that could pull small craft at tremendous speed.

"We can handle it," Larry said.

They practiced the spinnaker on their C-Lark. The process was simple—when traveling with the wind, take down the small jib and put up the spinnaker. The amount of power they got from the spinnaker, however, made the small boat instantly start to surf.

After a few minutes of sailing, Ann's arms started to burn from holding the spinnaker control arm and her legs were exhausted from exerting counter-balance against the much stronger pulling sail.

"This takes too much energy," Ann said. "The boat is too light." With a smaller boat, the ratio of crew to boat weight was close to even, requiring more activity from the crew to maintain top speeds.

"You're right." Larry scratched his chin. "People who finish tops in Working Sail are all pretty good athletes. We're getting older. Maybe we upgrade to a twenty-one foot San Juan. They're popular at the Yacht club." By getting a larger, heavier boat with a deeper keel, the boat itself could do more of the work to keep them on course. They would only need to provide the proper rigging and tactics.

They found one that was lime green on top with a white hull.

"We should call it *Peridot*," Ann said.

Larry had misheard her and answered, "Pair-a-dot? One time I hit another boat…" He trailed off, raising an eyebrow.

"No!" Ann laughed. "The boat is the color of a rare gemstone."

One of their first times racing the San Juan was at the Lake of the Woods. It was a high-wind day. With every turn, the *Peridot* seemed at the whim of the wind.

"The rudder's sluggish." Larry leaned on the tiller, but the boat continued to travel in the direction of the wind, only making wide, slow turns.

"Maybe it's the wind?" Ann scanned the rest of the regatta to see how the other boats were doing. On shore, a flag consisting of vertical white and red stripes was hoisted. "They're abandoning the race."

Larry was too focused on the tiller to notice.

"Larry!" Ann yelled over the howl of the wind.

"What?!"

Ann pointed to shore. Larry saw the white and red flag.

"Probably for the best, now we can figure out what's

wrong," he said.

As they neared shore, Ann went to crank the swing keel up. The crank didn't budge. Ann laughed. "We forgot to put down the centerboard!" Effectively, they were sailing without a keel, which was the larger boat's primary ballast to counter the strength of the wind, the way that Ann had been the ballast of their smaller boat by hiking over the gunwale. Without that ballast, the wind bullied *Peridot* through sloppy turns.

Larry shook his head. His face turned a deep shade of red, but before his legendary 'blue air' shouted out, his lips pulled wide and he guffawed along with her.

With the San Juan 21, Ann and Larry saw competition on the local circuit and added a few new races in Newport, at McNary Dam, and Whiskey Town in Northern California. Peridot always finished near the top of the leaderboard and won the B Class regionals at Howard Prairie. The following year they were invited to the Western Nationals at Huntington Lake near Fresno.

They arrived at the event after dark the night before the first race. When they checked at the Inn, the desk clerk had unfortunate news. "We're booked solid. I'm sorry. There's no room at the Inn."

Outside, Ann and Larry conferred.

"The next closest inn is several hours away," Ann said.

"It's too bad we didn't bring the old canvas tent." Larry scratched at his chin. "We could sleep on the boat."

"On the boat?"

"It has a berth and we have blankets." Larry grinned.

While it was pleasant on the lake during the day, at night, the temperatures dropped rapidly. The San Juan class of boats were constructed of fiberglass. The lightweight material lacked sufficient insulation to keep away the chill from the cold lake water.

"This isn't very comfortable," Ann said.

"We need to share our warmth," Larry said.

"I can hardly turn over. My hips keep hitting the top of the berth."

By morning, they were exhausted. Angry fatigue drove them to place first in every race. After suffering through another miserably cold night on the water, they placed first in their next two races. By noon on Sunday, they were tired, sore, and grateful to be off the water and lunching at the local yacht club with the National Commodore.

"I'm told you've clinched the B Class National Trophy," the Commodore said. A single shotgun blast sounded in the distance. The Commodore checked his watch. "I believe that's your last race." He looked up from his watch to see an empty table.

Ann and Larry sprinted all-out to the dock. "We've already won." Larry panted as he untied the boat. "They only keep our best five times."

"What if this one is better?" Ann asked.

Larry was thinking the same thing. By the time they reached the starting line they were ten minutes late. It took every trick they had amassed over a decade of sailing to place third in the final race. Their overall score was best in class. Encouraged by their B Class National Trophy, they upgraded their jib and spinnaker so they could compete in the A Class.

23

Lost at Sea
San Francisco 1978

There was no rain as Ann and Larry prepared *Peridot*, their San Juan 21 racing yacht, to depart Berkeley Yacht Harbor. "Forecast calls for high winds," Larry pulled an orange bag from below decks. "We should use storm sails, I think."

"Jib and main?" Ann more suggested than asked.

"Get to rigging." Larry tossed one bag to Ann and unpacked the second.

Once free of the harbor, they raised the bright orange storm sails that were a third the size of normal sails. With winds between 15 and 20 knots they didn't need to motor into the bay. Wind gusts frothed white caps and added chop to the water.

"No repeats of yesterday." Larry had guilt behind his eyes. He pointed to one of the buoys. "That's the one."

During the previous day's race they had been in tight pursuit of the leader only to finish without the bleat of the sounding horn. Race authority quickly told them that both they and the lead boat had missed that particular marker buoy. At the time, the heavy fog had made it difficult for them to find the errant marker. Their score for the day had been ruined.

"If we post a good time…we still have a chance at the top of the board," Larry said.

They followed the rest of the fleet to the rendezvous with the committee boat at the Olympic Circle just outside the Berkeley Marina. The circle was a ring of racing buoys situated every forty-five degrees along the circumference of a two nautical-mile diameter ring.

Photographers aboard the committee boat captured the gathered fleet of San Juan twenty-one-footers for the yacht club's news-sheet.

"Be sure to smile, dear," Ann teased.

"I am smiling." Larry's eyes squinted and his mustache covered upper lip was flatter than the undulating bay. He had taken to wearing the mustache to keep his lips from chapping while playing golf and sailing.

At the shotgun blast, they began the first leg of the race going West toward Angel Island.

"Storm clouds." Ann pointed to gathering grey clouds over the Golden Gate Bridge. She already wore rain clothes under her life-vest.

"At least it's not fog," Larry muttered. He gave Ann control of the tiller so he could also dress for the impending storm.

The Bay Bridge stretched across the port horizon. At a thirty-degree tack from their bow was the spec of an island known as Alcatraz. Directly ahead was *Red Boat*. The crimson ship had a heavier crew, and *Peridot* was in prime racing condition. The gap closed.

Lightning lit the sky. Thunder was challenged by wind and sea so all that reached Ann and Larry was an ominous growl.

By the third maker buoy, the rain came, bringing with it a squall filled with sudden and violent wind changes.

"*Red Boat* is lowering their sail!"

Larry could barely hear Ann for the noise of the wind whipping past his ears. The urgency of her repeated point, however, caused him to squint against the rain. He saw the main sail go down. "Yes. Let's do that too!"

They let both their sails go, lowering the jib and main as fast as they could. Waves grew to six feet. The El Niñõ conditions already had raised the tides in the San Francisco Bay. The warmer than normal seawater was less dense and easier for the violent wind to shape and change.

Larry tightened his grip on the tiller as a wave crashed over the bow of the *Red Boat*, completely submerging the twenty-one footer. The wave crossed the fifty yards to *Peridot*. Larry couldn't think of anything else to say but an instinctual, "Look out!"

Larry tried to steer into the wave, but it came too fast for a correction and the wave struck *Peridot* on the port side. He saw Ann knocked clear of the boat—jumping or thrown he couldn't tell—then there was cold, salty water everywhere. The wave passed over him.

He blinked stinging saltwater from his eyes. Where was Ann?

Another wave rushed the boat. These weren't ocean swells caused by far off storms, but instead a series of rapid and onerous waves fed by the raging gusts of wind of the storm surge. *Peridot*, even with its deep keel, was no match for the turmoil of the water and the next wave completely submerged the small craft and Larry.

He was entombed in a buoyant darkness. Water. Cold.

His body turned and tumbled. No air. His lungs burned. He kicked for the surface but didn't move. Something had his leg. He kicked again. The force was great. He reached down and felt a line wrapped around his foot. His lungs began to burn. The waves pulled at him, up and down, side to side, all the while he pulled and strained at the line until his foot was free. He kicked. When he breached the surface it wasn't to sky: the boat's cabin. He gasped for air.

The waves were relentless assailants against the sideways boat. Each of their strikes flushed salty air through the cabin. Larry saw a floating towel, which he stuffed back in its place. The course maps, spare life jacket...he continued to place things back into their homes. He was deep in the grip of shock. He took a moment to breathe. His mind cleared enough for one thought: "ANN!"

Several minutes earlier, the wind gusts had knocked Ann from her feet. She huddled next to the gunwale, clutching the teak rail. When the waves grew too violent and the boat began to roll, the sails came straight towards her. Even the small storm sails were big enough to trap her. On instinct she kicked free of the boat before it capsized.

Waves rolled her. For a moment she couldn't tell which way was up. Was she under the boat? Drowning? She opened her eyes to a salty stinging blackness. There— light. She kicked and fought to the surface.

Waves besieged her. Where was the shore? Where was the boat?

"Larry!" she yelled but all she heard in response was the howl of wind and rush of water around her.

Ann treaded water and turned in frantic circles. Where

was *Peridot*? Where was *Red Boat*?

"Larry!"

No answer. Ann felt crushing fear. This was how she would die. Alone at sea, lost and drowned in a storm.

Lightning flashed. She saw something angular against the water. It must be a boat. It had to be. Ann estimated it was at least two city blocks away. Nothing to do but swim for it. It would be too far to crawl. She rolled on her back and began to kick. Rain and water continued to pelt her face. Her eyes were slits as she closed on the listing boat.

"LARRY!"

He scrambled to the hatch and pulled himself free to sea. The waves had thrown *Peridot* to its side. With the keel above the surface and mast below water, the craft was unable to self-right. Larry looked for any place to stand on the sideways boat and finally settled on the mast. He scanned in every direction on the roiling sea before finally seeing orange. A life-vest! Ann back floated against the waves.

"ANN!"

She kicked and pulled with her arms. Waves smashed over her. Larry lost sight of her. "Ann!" When she surfaced near the *Peridot*, Larry grabbed her with one hand and held the mast with his other.

Ann coughed up bay water. She grabbed the door to the cabin.

"Things are floating out!" Ann yelled.

"What!?"

"I can feel them against my legs!"

Larry looked aft towards the cabin. Among other things, the rudder had come dislodged from the boat and floated towards the approaching committee ship.

Following the rudder were the sail-bags for the fair weather main sail, jib, and spinnaker.

"Hold tight!" the voice came from starboard. Larry looked. It was the committee boat.

"Get us out of here!" Larry yelled.

"We can't come close! The water's too turbulent! Is everyone accounted for?"

"Yes! We're both here!" Larry yelled back.

"Wait for the Coast Guard!" The committee ship motored off against the waves. The nearby *Red Boat* had fared worse than *Peridot* and was completely capsized with its mast straight down. Larry could see someone hanging to the centerboard keel while another floated limp against the waves. The committee boat fished him out of the water.

Rain turned to hail. Wind whipped spray horizontally.

By the time the Coast Guard Motor Response Boat reached them, Larry's fingers had gone completely numb.

A bull-horn amplified voice called out to them: "Is everyone out of the boat?"

"Yes!" Larry yelled.

The chop was great and the Coast Guard had to make several attempts to close the gap with the beleaguered *Peridot*. When near enough, the Coast Guard threw an orange and white striped life ring to them.

"Let's go!" Larry yelled to Ann.

"We can't leave the boat!"

"We're freezing! There's nothing to do for the boat!"

Ann relented. The two of them grabbed the life ring and were hauled through the turbulent waters to the waiting Coast Guard rescue boat. Ann was hauled aboard first. Larry gripped the ladder on the end of the boat. He pulled. His arms had no strength left. It was all he could do to hang on. A pair of Coast Guard hands pulled Larry and his five layers of soaking wet clothing onto the ship.

A mate led them belowdeck. "Get out of your wet things and get under blankets."

They shed down to underwear and wrapped themselves in wool blankets. Larry couldn't stop shivering.

"I can hear your teeth chattering," Ann said.

Larry tried to grin, but couldn't.

A few minutes later, two crew members from the *Red Boat* joined them in the below decks. The radio crackled above deck. It was difficult to make out what was said. "Cardiac event…Treasure Island…Hospital." They referenced the limp crew-member from the *Red Boat* who had been pulled from the turbulent bay.

The Coast Guard sped them to the Berkeley Yacht Club. Ann and the crew of the *Red Boat* were rushed to the hot showers. Larry wrung out his jogging clothes and pulled them on.

"You should shower," one of the Coast Guard mates said.

"I'll be fine. Ann's going to need warm clothes. Can you give me a lift to my car?"

The mate did.

Larry changed into dry clothes in the parking lot and drove back. He loaned what clothes he could to the crew of the *Red Boat* while Ann dressed in warm clothes. The group of them convened in the galley where gas burners warmed them.

"It feels good in here," Larry attempted to make conversation.

"Hot coffee," Ann said. She took a mug for herself and

one for Larry.

By 2PM, the Coast Guard pulled the *Peridot* back to harbor. Larry helped the Coast Guard mates to bail out and balance the boat back on its trailer. When Larry tried to pull it up the ramp, his tires just spun. One of the Coast Guard had a 4x4 and helped to pull the boat from the water.

In the parking lot, Larry removed the seawater logged cushions, removed and straightened the mast, and bailed what water he could. He even found Ann's purse at the rear of the boat along with the fire extinguisher and tool kit.

That night, they hung wet clothes around their hotel room. Ann's purse had carried several days worth of spending money. Those bills were hung alongside their clothes.

During both the 6PM and 11PM news broadcasts, Larry winced as he saw photos of *Peridot* being pulled from the harbor with its mast bent at an awkward forty-five degree angle. The reporter described that three boats had capsized and two, *Golden Dragon* & *Peppermint* had sailed off without a crew. At the end of the newscast, the reporter asked him what he would do differently next time. Larry said, "We hope there is no next time. Once is enough."

24

Thank you Goodbye
Coos Bay 1979

Merl Howard brought an opportunity to Larry's attention. "It's in Coos Bay. The Lake Empire Apartments."

While Larry frequently raced sailboats in Coos Bay, he needed to walk the site to know if the location would work. What did the neighborhood sound like? What smells were there? How was traffic and access to amenities? He drove to the site. It was a couple short blocks from the south end of Upper Empire Lake, with easy access from the adjoining major street. Once on the property, he began to visualize the final project. Pine trees dominated the area, and the fresh crisp breeze blowing off the lake invigorated Larry. He agreed to take a 25% stake in the project.

Quite a few trees were going to be destroyed to prepare the lot for construction. Larry decided to conserve as many as he could. He dug up the small trees, those that he could reasonably carry and brought them back to Medford to plant in the front yard of his house.

The Empire Lake Apartments were completed in 1980

with $70,000 in cost overruns due to issues with labor, contractors, and inferior siding that warped and had to be replaced. The location proved to be farther away than Larry was comfortable traveling to manage. When Merle Howard decided he wanted out of the apartments, Larry convinced Craig to buy into them so they could split management duties.

Larry searched for ideal locations closer to home. When an Ashland lumber mill went into foreclosure, Larry attempted to buy some of the land from Jackson County. The Ashland City Planner, however, had designated the area as a park. Larry tried to re-zone the land, feeling the location would be wasted on a park. However, his attempts to turn the land into low-income housing were stopped by the Ashland City Council.

Larry commiserated with Ann: "The Ashland site isn't going to work."

"Why not?" Ann asked.

"The city only wants low-income housing, but the rules of section eight were changed. The government is only giving grants to non-profits."

"Could you make a non-profit?" Ann asked.

"The whole idea is that I'm in this for a profit," Larry said. "Getting traditional apartments approved by the city just isn't going to happen right now."

A few years later, the City of Ashland took ownership of the lot and built low-income housing on the site. Meanwhile, the Marquess group entered into a partnership with a land-owner on Table Rock Road. They presented a proposal to Medford Planning Commission.

"The road is too busy," was the response.

"There's a need for low-income housing in the area,"

Larry argued.

"Your project isn't going to get approved." Just like Ashland, Medford Planning Commission was pushing for non-profits. While forming a non-profit could benefit land developers—they still got paid for the construction—the ownership structure prohibited investors like Larry from being able to gain profit. The Marquess group sold their stake in the land to a local non-profit, the Housing Authority of Jackson County. With the State of Oregon's backing, the land was re-zoned, and the project was approved.

"I had a good plan," Larry told Ann, "but it looks like the landscape is changing."

"It really is a shame," Ann said. "How many did we end up with?"

"Two hundred, thirteen, and a half units."

"A half?"

"Yes, but it's the good half," Larry joked.

Larry and Ann owned 18 units at Takilma Village, 32 at Chief Tyee, 56 at Julia Ann, 24 of the 36 at T'Morrow for the Elderly, 36 at Northwood, 8 of the 40 at Eastwood, 8.5 of the 17 at Johnston Manor, and 21 of the 28 at Lake Empire, plus an additional 10 condos. Larry's investment income was $115,000 per year, or $337,000 in 2017 dollars.

"I'm making three times my Marquess income," Larry said. "Maybe it's time to retire…"

To make the transition to retirement easier, Larry decided to sell some of his property. He wanted to be rid of any problem properties so he would have more time for travel and leisure. Takilma Village was starting to show its age, making it an easy property to sell, and managing

Lake Empire from a distance made that one undesirable as well.

On April 1, 1985, Larry retired from Marquess and Associates at the age of 58. It's unclear just who the April Fools Day prank was against as Larry continued his electrical engineering consulting and began working daily to supervise his investment property portfolio. A strong work ethic was ingrained in Larry. He knew deep down that he would work as long as he was able.

25

Getting Back on the Boat
Eugene 1980

Larry and Ann launched *Peridot* at the Fern Ridge Reservoir outside of Eugene. High gusts caught the sail and made the boat lean. Ann slipped her feet into the hiking straps and gripped the teak handrail. Her breathing came faster. She closed her eyes and remembered being thrown from the boat, lost amid six-foot waves, unable to find reference of land or ship. Just her and water.

"Easy," Larry said.

Ann blinked her eyes open. Sunlight glinted off white caps. She looked at Larry.

"Don't worry, we're not going over," Larry said.

"It seems like we're always tipping over," Ann said.

Larry, sensing Ann's trepidation, wasn't as aggressive as usual. He made wide corrections so that Ann wouldn't have to hike over the edge of the boat and took slow but steady jibs with the wind directly at their back. They only beat a couple boats.

"Not our best finish," Larry said.

"The wind came up. I got uneasy." Ann grimaced.

While loading their boat onto the trailer, they heard two

distant blasts.

"Sounds like military maneuvers," Larry said. He'd heard plenty of ordinance detonations while practicing his marksmanship at Camp Pendleton.

On the road back to Medford, they listened to the radio. "Mount St. Helens has just erupted. The cone-shaped peak that overlooked Clark County has just exploded with force like an atom bomb. Half of the volcano is gone. The death toll is unknown at this time." It was the single most devastating volcanic eruption in the history of the lower 48 states, causing over a billion dollars in damage, decimating the mountain, and killing more than fifty people.

Ann's fingers white knuckled on the door handle. "That was the boom we heard. The death toll…" Ann looked out the window.

"Something wrong?" Larry asked.

"On the water today, I kept thinking of the San Francisco Bay. I'm lucky to be alive." Ann closed her eyes and again remembered the grey San Francisco sky with its pelting rain, the stinging spray from whitecaps, and the ominous feeling of being lost at sea.

Larry nodded. "Maybe we try casual sailing for a while?"

"That might be good."

They decided on an overnight sail on Klamath Lake. Between the lake's shallow depth and valley location, the surface was generally placid. Larry hoped it would ease Ann back into sailing.

The first day was a sail north to Rocky Point, an unincorporated region where they anchored for the night. By morning, they sailed back the other way, to the main body of the upper Klamath Lake. During the sail they were besieged by 'noseeums'—sand flies that swarmed the lake's surface.

Larry bellowed instruction to set the sail. He started coughing.

"Something wrong?" Ann swiveled.

"I got bugs in my mouth." Larry tried to spit them out.

"I guess you have to keep your mouth shut." As soon as Ann said it, she regretted it, as several bugs swarmed into her mouth as well. She was as ineffective at spitting them out as Larry; the tiny insects stuck to her tongue.

Without much wind, they drifted across the lake. Because of the bugs, they couldn't talk, so they listened to the radio.

"Are people already at the congregation spot?" Ann blurted it without thinking of the bugs.

Larry looked. He covered his mouth and said, "Yes."

Ann spat several sand flies out, then likewise covered her mouth. "How did they get there so fast?"

They questioned the early arrivers when they pulled alongside.

"We got tired of drifting, so we used our motors," one of them said.

On the way back to Medford, Larry asked, "How was the sail?"

"Fine."

"You don't sound excited."

"I miss racing," Ann said. "There was none of this… cheating with a motor."

Larry laughed. "Are you up for it?"

"Kind of the thing…if you fall off a horse, you have to get back on." Ann managed an uncertain smile.

"Western Nationals are on Lake Washington this year," Larry said. "It should be smoother sailing than San Francisco…there's still time to qualify."

"Let's try," Ann said.

They returned to the Southern Oregon regatta circuit. The lakes were familiar old friends with sheltering mountains on all sides. Instead of dealing with waves, they dealt with juts of land and fickle winds. Racing under these conditions gave Ann small doses of confidence. All that changed when they returned to Tenmile lake near Coos Bay.

Coastal winds made the water choppy and rocked *Peridot* as they cranked down the centerboard. Ann gripped the teak gunwale until her hand cramped.

"We'll be fine," Larry said.

"Just don't dunk me," Ann said.

"That was years ago, in a smaller boat," Larry said. *Peridot* was much more resilient to capsize than their earlier *Bluit* or *Blue Air*.

Midway through the race, coastal gusts battered their boat. Ann dug her feet deeper under the hiking straps. She grit her teeth. Closing her eyes, she remembered the orange storm sails falling towards her on the San Francisco bay. She opened her eyes. White sails and a billowing orange spinnaker. Sun. Blue sky. Clear water rushed by the gunwales.

"Are you okay?" Larry asked.

"Just win," Ann said. Winning was more important than fear. And each win gave Ann more confidence for the next race. Her and Larry applied everything they knew of sailing. Their nervous energy from memories of San Francisco fueled them to place at the top of their division.

Western Nationals were held on Lake Washington, a long lake that formed the eastern border of Seattle. The lake itself was a glacier carved ribbon lake. Ann and Larry frequently sailed the dendritic lake at Coos Bay, giving them expertise and skill navigating close to land. They were in third as they entered the leg that ran downwind across the deepest part of the lake.

"We can catch them!" Larry yelled. "You gotta hike."

Ann double checked her feet were secure under the hiking strap. She held the gunwale and leaned. Wind pulled the spinnaker taut. Caps of water rushed by underneath. Gusts rocked them, bringing Ann's face within inches of the water. She held tight to the hand grips.

"We're catching them!"

Ann watched as they gained on the second place boat. Another gust rocked the *Peridot*, tilting it farther. Ann held to the boat and kept her body stiff as the water raced up to meet her. She got dunked. Her eyes squeezed shut. The cold rushed over her. Her hat was pulled free. She heard nothing. Saw nothing. This was a watery tomb. Then she was in the air. Water streamed across her face. She gulped for breath, opened her eyes to wet strands of hair crossing her face, and screamed.

"Ann!" Larry yelled.

"I'm okay! Race!" She held tight to the boat, adrenaline burning through her.

The second place boat got too close to shore and lost its wind. *Peridot* slipped past it, getting right of way for the buoy turn. The other boat was forced to back off. *Peridot* cut a tight line through the white caps and closed on the first place boat.

"They fumbled their tack!" Ann yelled.

"We can beat them. Fast! Fast!" Larry bellowed.

Ann unhiked and crossed the ship to the jib and mainsail. She rigged swiftly on instinct. They kept their speed.

A boom echoed across the lake.

"What was that?" Ann yelled.

"Just hike!" Larry yelled.

Ann ignored the boom and locked her feet into the hiking strap. She leaned. Their boat hydroplaned across the water towards the finish line, passing the leader. They were first for this race.

"I think that was the best race we ever had," Ann said.

"It looks like you're ready for high winds again," Larry said.

"Yes, I suppose I am."

They finished fourth overall for the regatta—their second fourth place in Northwest Finals. They later learned the boom was Mt. St. Helens. This time it was a dome building eruption that released massive plumes of ash into the air.

Their drive back on I-5 was delayed. The fine ash clogged air filters and destroyed the engines of running cars, so Ann and Larry waited overnight for it to settle. As a powdery layer of ash formed outside, Larry went out with a jar.

"What are you doing?" Ann asked.

He scooped ash from the bumpers of several parked cars. He came back to Ann with a grin on his face. "We can use this to take roughness off the boat finish—more speed!"

Ann laughed. She felt the call of racing once again. When Ann and Larry finally retired from racing, they had accumulated over 110 trophies which decorated their home.

26

Expansion!
Medford 1983

Lawrence's Jewelers had an unexpected visitor who met with Ann, Bob, Chuck and Jerry. He was a leasing officer for a development company responsible for filling spaces in the up and coming Rogue Valley Mall. After the meeting, the four family members met to discuss the opportunity.

Chuck led off: "Last Thanksgiving I was in Bend. The mall was packed. This kind of foot traffic could pay for an entire year. This is the future."

Bob shook his head. "No. The rents are too high. We'll never sell enough."

"The downtown store isn't doing enough business to support four families. This could be a good opportunity for me," Chuck said.

"It's a no," Bob said.

A few months later, Chuck met with Ann and Larry over dinner. He had news to share: "The initial developers went under. The new ones have a proposal for a less extravagant mall with lower rates. I think we could make this happen."

Larry was interested by Chuck's excitement. It was the era of Ronald Reagan, and there seemed to be business opportunities everywhere Larry looked. While Larry had been mentoring Craig in property investment and management, he now had an opportunity to help two of his other sons in an entrepreneurial endeavor. He checked Ann's interest with a simple question: "Do you remember that jewelry store in Pocatello?"

"The family business, yes. They had a store downtown and a mall store."

"The mall store did more business," Larry said.

Ann nodded in agreement.

"Let's work the numbers. We can see if the idea is viable. How good are you at spreadsheets?" Larry asked Chuck.

Historically, Larry did his calculations on actual spreadsheets—pages with columns and rows that allowed for a quick glance at finances. With the rise of the personal computer and Lotus 1-2-3, suddenly spreadsheets became interactive. While this was baby steps compared to the power of modern spreadsheet programs, it was enough that they could quickly crunch numbers to determine the sales required to cover costs and make the venture viable. Among other things, Larry introduced Chuck to double entry bookkeeping, and financial foresight...how a small change now can make a big change over time.

"You have to control your expenses," Larry said.

"How do you do that?" Chuck asked.

"You have fixed expenses, like lease payments. You have to get that right, because you can't change it later. Half of making money is buying—or leasing—at the right rate.

But this is a retail business. You'll have other expenses, like payroll, unturned inventory. Those can be more liquid. You can scale those as necessary. Get the right lease terms, and this can be a really profitable venture."

Larry accompanied Chuck to pitch the idea to Jerry, Ann and Bob.

"I'm not interested in a mall store," Bob said.

"Before you say no, everyone should take a look at this," Chuck said. He began his presentation of the spreadsheets and analysis that he and Larry had worked on.

By the end of the presentation, Jerry said, "I'd be interested in going there to do gold-smithing."

"We could put you in the front window to get people's interest," Chuck said.

"I don't know," Bob said.

"If we don't go there, someone else will," Chuck said.

Larry glanced back and forth between the two of them. Chuck's enthusiasm was infectious. Larry wanted to see how far this new venture could go. "Bob, let's talk it out." He led Bob into the back office for a private discussion.

Bob explained: "This is a lot of risk—risking what I worked my whole life for."

"It'll be no risk to you. Ann and I can fund the whole venture," Larry said. "But…it would be more successful with the Lawrence's name. That's a brand you helped build. You'd get a stake in the business."

"No financial risk?" Bob raised an eyebrow.

"Leave that to me."

"Deal."

The Rogue Valley Mall opened in the fall of 1986. Lawrence's II had a ten year lease with an option for an additional five years. Chuck and Jerry entered into a partnership, C&J Enterprises. When the doors first opened, Larry went to visit the new store.

"A lot of foot traffic." Larry motioned to the crowds in the mall.

"Not a lot of bags going out the door," Chuck reported, "I thought it would be like downtown. Open the doors and people come in and you ask, 'what do you want?' and you sell it to them."

"What are you doing to fix it?" Larry asked.

"I'm going to bring in some sales training specialists. We can turn this around," Chuck said.

"Would more inventory help?" Larry asked.

"It might. It just might."

"I'll talk to Ann and Bob. They have more inventory than they can show. We'll work an agreement out," Larry said. "Beyond that, I can give you a line of credit."

Lawrence's II went on to borrow $87,000 from Larry to fund startup inventory. Between that and consignment inventory from downtown, the store's sales picked up. By Christmas, the store was profitable. Several years later Larry was able to help the store cut costs again by paying off the store's $160,000 loan from Crater Bank, and offering a lower interest rate to Chuck and Jerry.

With that refinancing, the store's profitability boomed. They had excess cashflow which inspired Chuck and Jerry to bring a new proposal to Larry.

"We have a lot of people coming from Ashland," Jerry said.

"We thought, why not take the store to them?" Chuck proposed.

Larry nodded. This fit his investment strategy. Start small, find something that works and repeat. "What do you need from me?"

By the time Lawrence's Jewelers III opened, the debt owed to Larry was up to $557,000. People from Ashland continued to shop at the Mall as the location in Ashland was too far from Lithia Plaza to get tourist foot traffic. Lawrence's III closed its doors in less than a year. It would take Lawrence's II several years to recover from that financial blow and pay Larry back. Larry took it in stride. He remembered their investment in the restaurant. It had been a hard lesson, but it had stuck: Not every investment worked out, but you couldn't have a winner without taking risks.

27

Burglarized
March 18 1983

Larry and Ann entered the conference room at the Rogue Valley Country Club a few minutes before 7PM for the monthly Medford Apartment Owners meeting. For the next two hours the meeting covered changes in regulations for Medford Apartments, the current housing need in the Rogue Valley, and upcoming ballot measures that could impact future business. The meeting was scheduled to run until 10PM, but ended an hour early.

"Just how I like meetings, informative and over early," Larry said.

They enjoyed a leisurely drive home in Larry's El Camino.

"We're nearly the largest individual rental owners in the valley," Larry said. "All we need is one more big project and I think we will be." Larry drummed his fingers on the steering wheel.

Changing the subject, Ann asked, "How's your father doing?"

"Not good," Larry said. "He hasn't recovered from the strokes and has been getting weaker all year. He can still get around a little with the help of a walker, but he talks very little. Mother—Retta—is doing a fine job taking care of him." Larry shook his head. "He still recognizes me, but I don't know how much longer he's going to last."

Dealing with a dying father brought mortality to the forefront of Larry's mind. When Marty had died, he had been devastated, but her death had been a complication of a brain tumor while his father was dying of age. This planted a seed in the back of Larry's mind that he needed to get everything out of his last good years that he could.

Larry was somber as he pulled into the driveway at their Barneburg house. His transplanted trees from the Empire Lake Apartments were growing well. The three bedroom house itself was modest considering the size of Larry's rental empire.

Larry went in first while Ann got the mail. As Larry flipped on the lights in the entryway, he heard a clanging in the kitchen. "Who's there?" He wondered if one of the boys had let themselves in. He glanced around, but none of the lights were on in the house. He heard the door to the back porch swinging. Larry tongued the inside of his cheek. Someone was here. He needed something. In the closet next to the door, he found his clubs. He took the pitching wedge. Smaller than the driver, it would be easier to swing in the tight confines of the house.

Ann came to the door. Larry held out a hand, palm open. "I think someone's inside." She stood on the porch step.

Armed with the iron, Larry, investigated. The door to the back patio was ajar. He checked room by room, turning on the lights, looking behind doors, under beds, in closets. Once he had searched the entire house, he brought Ann in.

"Check to see if anything's missing," he said.

A few minutes later, they met in the kitchen.

"All my jewelry's gone," Ann said.

"So are my guns, and that bronze sculpture of an eagle from the living room," Larry said.

They called the police. A detective came by to take their statements. After telling him what they knew was gone, Ann added: "They didn't get the silver."

Larry scratched at a sudden itch on the back of his neck. "We must have surprised them. The meeting was advertised to run later than it did."

The detective thanked them for their statements and warned them that stolen jewelry and firearms were often very difficult to find and recover, as they would all likely be pawned out of town.

Insurance estimates on the heist came out around $50,000 in 2017 dollars. They had the back door to the patio reinforced with dead bolts and added an exterior lighting system and alarm from SOS. Even with these precautions, Larry became a light sleeper, waking at any bump in the night.

Gene later died from pneumonia on December 7th, 1983, the 42nd anniversary of the attack on Pearl Harbor.

28

Ann and the GIA
Medford 1984

Ann wrapped a vase. Wood-inspired grains gave texture to the shiny, heavy paper that had become an icon of Lawrence's. Ann folded expert corners from years of practice as she looked around the store. Elsie was busy with the books in the overlook office. Bob was hard at work resetting a stone in a ring—the rise of the quartz watch was slowly making his skills as a watchmaker obsolete. Jerry was at the bench in the back of the shop, engraving silver for a customer. They had seen a demonstration of a computer that could engrave with Jerry's accuracy, but not with his speed or artistic flourish.

Ann's role as buyer had grown from gifts to housewares and now included some jewelry. Still, her primary responsibility at the store was working as a clerk. That included sales, tracking customer purchase records for warrant work, and wrapping gifts. This time she did a two-color ribbon—red and green for the approaching Christmas.

Bows were made in advance during Thanksgiving bow-making parties at Elsie's house. They had a hand-cranked machine that could turn out a bow a minute. After one night, they had enough bows to make it through the busy holiday season. If they ran out early, they would have to wind bows by hand, a time consuming process that could back up sales. Ann tied this bow to the ribbon.

Ann began to butterfly the hidden loops of ribbon out and wondered what she could do to improve the store's bottom line. Where was a need at Lawrence's she could fill? Ann could grow her buying to include gems for the store—Bob wouldn't have to vacate his bench to go on buying trips. To do that, she would have to learn more about gems, something that would help her duties as a clerk as well. Ann liked that idea.

By the time each of the hidden loops of ribbon had been pulled and twisted, the homemade ribbon looked bigger and plumper than factory produced ribbons. Ann handed the wrapped gift to the customer.

"What about the pinecone? You didn't run out, did you?" The woman raised her eyebrows in horror.

"No, no, I just forgot." Ann laughed. She had been distracted with thoughts of gems. A moment later, she tied one of the signature pinecones to the bow—Arnel's contribution that never left the store.

The customer beamed.

Ann approached Bob. "You did the GIA courses, right?" She asked.

"Yes. Why do you ask?"

"I think I might like to do them too."

"Are we going to need a third repair bench?" Bob laughed. He nodded his head towards the back where Jerry worked a couple days a week doing engraving. The mall store didn't have an engraving bench, so Jerry had to travel downtown to complete engraving for both stores.

"I don't want anyone else to know more about jewelry than I do. It'll make me a better clerk. And you won't have to go on buying trips anymore."

"I like the sound of that," Bob said. "You know, they offer correspondence courses. You could learn while you work."

Ann did. In the late 1980s, Ann took courses from the GIA. She learned to grade diamonds, gems, and colored stones. Part of the class covered repairs, although Ann left that area to Bob and Jerry. At the end of each course, Ann was tested at the Medford library and earned several certificates for grading. To complete an appraisal, she had to set a price based on grade against the current market conditions.

Over time, grading gems became more complicated, as manufacturers discovered the recipes to mimic natural stones: a combination of mineral ingredients and the temperatures and pressures necessary to bind them together. While these synthetic stones were often expensive to manufacture, they sold for less than the more rare natural stones. GIA courses helped Ann learn to tell the difference between a highly sought after naturally occurring gem, and a mass-produced synthetic that could fool the uneducated.

Every time she learned something new, she passed the knowledge on to Chuck and Jerry.

"Gems are so beautiful and interesting," she told them. "I just marvel that nature makes so many beautiful things. You can look at something and think it's a citrine, but it doesn't have the right elements. Gem identification is like a detective story. You have to follow the scientific steps, find the clues to the truth of the gem." She loved it so much that she bought Chuck and Jerry a course in diamonds from the GIA. Lawrence's II became known for its customer education on the four 'C's of diamonds: Cut, Color, Clarity, and Carat.

29

Fountain Plaza
Medford 1988

Jane's voice buzzed on the intercom: "Larry, your 10AM is here."

Larry glanced to the clock. 9:55AM. Five minutes early, off to a good start, Larry thought. To the intercom, he said, "Send him in."

The man who walked in had the wide shouldered gait of a man who worked construction most of his life—as a laborer and later as a contractor.

"Bob, good to see you again," Larry said.

"Larry, it's a pleasure," Bob Youngs said.

They shook hands.

"Tell me about this proposal," Larry said.

"Medford needs another retirement home." Bob grinned. Larry nodded. It was well known that the only full-service retirement home in town—the Manor was failing to meet demand.

"I've got just the spot for it too." Bob handed across a sheaf of papers. The cover page read: Fountain Plaza.

Larry flipped through the pages. "Where is this?" The photocopy of the map was difficult to read. Squinting didn't help.

"Berrydale. It's off Table Rock Road," Bob said.

"It's too far out for services," Larry said. "Retired people won't want to drive that far." He flipped through a few more pages.

"But you're interested in the project?" Bob asked.

Larry sighed. "Let me sleep on this one." He drove out to Berrydale to walk the potential site. A big sawmill—MedCO—was a couple blocks away. The smell from the mill was terrible. All around the site were large industrial lots. Larry couldn't imagine anyone wanting to live here. By morning, he'd reached a decision and called Bob to deliver the bad news, "I'm going to pass on this one. I just don't like your location."

Larry thought that was the end of his involvement with Fountain Plaza until he got another call from Bob several months later. He had put together a new proposal for a facility next to T'Morrow for the Elderly.

Bob Youngs needed Larry's help to secure the site. "Can you get the land from Charles Gorr?" Bob asked. "He said to talk to you—that you had an arrangement to trade the land for equity in T'Morrow for the Elderly."

Larry considered this surprise offer. Charles Gorr had previously been a 1/3 owner in T'Morrow for the Elderly before medical expenses had driven him to sell out his ownership to Larry. "So you want Charles's land. And he wants part of T'Morrow. How much money can you give me for it?"

"We can pay you once we get a loan approved," Bob said.

"How are you going to finance the project?" Larry asked.

"We have a financial backer in Beverly Hills," Bob said.

Larry raised an eyebrow at this. "That's a long ways off. Something tells me, you want local finances."

Bob moved his mouth like he was chewing on something, or licking the inside of his lip. At some length, he said, "Is that a possibility?"

"The world is made up of possibilities," Larry said. "Tell me more about the project."

Bob grinned. He opened up a folder and took out a glossy covered proposal in color. Bob started a well-rehearsed pitch: "It's a one-hundred and twenty unit facility with some residential care features. This style of retirement home has become red-hot in California. As people are trying to find a more affordable lifestyle, communities in Oregon are becoming more desirable. Communities like right here, in Medford."

Bob flipped to a page showing blueprints of a facility. "I've already built several of these before. They all made money. This is going to change Medford forever."

"What would you need from an investor?" Larry felt the old tickle of opportunity in the back of his mind. It had been years since Section 8 changes had shifted low-income housing to Housing Authorities. If these retirement homes were as lucrative as Bob suggested, Larry felt he might finally have a way to get back into becoming a serious real-estate investor.

"Can you secure finances?" Bob asked. "Charles tells me you own a considerable amount of rental units."

"Between my wife and I, we have two-hundred and seventeen subsidized apartments and half a jewelry store," Larry said.

"That just might do it," Bob said.

"Might?" Larry asked.

"This is a six million dollar project," Bob said. "If you can finance that…" he trailed off. "Between financing and the land. I could give you fifty-percent ownership." Bob's eyes flicked up to make contact with Larry's.

"You're donating your time?" Larry asked.

"I'd need to be paid for my work, of course," Bob said.

"Then I'd want to be paid for my land. And interest on any loans I have to make. Fifty percent ownership for access to the land and financial backing to make the project happen," Larry said.

Bob nodded. "That would work."

"Good," Larry said, "Let me do my due diligence. If everything checks out…we have a deal." They stood and exchanged handshakes.

As part of his due diligence, Larry ordered credit checks on Bob Youngs and wrote letters to the provided references. When letters of recommendation and credit checks came in, Larry Ann, and Craig reviewed them.

"The letters all have good recommendations," Larry said.

"I don't know very many people who provide bad references," Craig said.

Larry shrugged. "I think it's enough for me to go on."

"Don't do it," Craig said.

"Why not?"

"You're the only one putting up collateral—you're taking on all the risk. If something goes wrong, you could lose the apartments, everything," Craig said.

Larry thought on it a moment. He and Ann had excess cashflow and unused equity in their apartment buildings. That equated to millions of dollars worth of untapped credit. Larry could continue to let the credit go to waste, or he could utilize it for financial gain. He glanced to Ann. "Those retirement homes we visited in Portland appeared financially worthwhile," Larry said.

"Our mothers should have some retirement time in a place that nice," Ann said.

Larry looked back to Craig who shook his head a single time, *no*.

Larry couldn't stand the thought of missing an opportunity. "I'm going to do it anyway," Larry said, "Call the attorney. Have him put together a partnership agreement. Let's have our agent, Cox put together an application with the State of Oregon Housing Authority."

It wasn't long before the State of Oregon Housing Authority approved a long term housing loan at 9%. For the next phase, easements had to be secured and the land re-zoned for multi-family.

Charles Gorr became an unexpected stumbling block.

"I won't sign," Charles said.

"We had a deal," Larry said.

"Yes, a deal to trade land for fifty percent ownership in T'Morrow. It doesn't seem like a good idea to allow easements on my land," Charles said.

"That was the whole point of the deal. To make way for this new facility," Larry said.

"That wasn't part of the contract," Charles said.

"The contract was written long before we brought this deal up. We talked about this as part of the—"

"It's not written in the contract," Charles maintained.

"This doesn't feel like a very effective partnership," Larry said. "One of us is going to have to buy the other out."

Larry ordered an appraisal of T'Morrow for the Elderly, which came back at $800,000. He'd have to come up with half of that money to buy out Charles. However, he and the Youngs had previously agreed that the land was worth just under three-hundred thousand. Already it appeared Larry was going to have to take on an additional hundred thousand of financial exposure before even securing a construction loan.

Larry met with a broker with Medford State Bank.

"This is a bigger loan than we can cover," the broker said.

"Do you know anyone who can?" Larry asked.

"I used to work for a bank up in Portland, Security Pacific. You've already lined up long term financing. You have a solid financial statement. I'll tell them they'd be crazy not to take this loan."

The broker made a call while Larry waited. When the broker hung up the phone, he looked somberly at Larry. "This is what he said: 'Yeah, we'll take it at twelve percent.'" The broker and Larry exchanged grins. "But there's a catch. They only want to do five million."

"The project's six million!" Larry said.

The broker shrugged. "If you can find an extra million, then you got yourself a project."

Larry spent weeks reviewing his banking and finances before arranging for a $500,000 loan from the Valley of the Rogue Bank, a $450,000 second mortgage from US National Bank on his Northwood Apartments, and a $200,000 line of credit against his Valley of the Rogue Bank stocks. By the end of construction, Larry had loaned Fountain Plaza a million and a quarter dollars.

The first resident moved in during the month of June,

1991 with the official Open House held on July 25th, 1991.

"Happy 65th, dear," Ann told him at the party.

"What a celebration!" Larry looked around the newly constructed dining room. The chandelier was from Kusak, one of Ann's favorite vendors of cut glass. A reef aquarium was just outside the dining room. Windows lining the dining room looked out to the grand entry, where a five-spout, thirty foot diameter fountain sprayed water into the air. The food for the celebration came from what Larry considered the best cooking team in Jackson County. Medford had never seen a building like it. "We're really going to do well with this one," Larry said.

30

The Waters Run Red
Medford 1991

Permanent financing was put in place for Fountain Plaza on September 25th. The State of Oregon's six million dollar loan repaid the banks, paid Larry for the land, Bob Youngs and his son for their work, and Larry for his engineering. However, the loan didn't cover the project's more than four-hundred thousand dollars in cost overruns. More financially worrisome than that, Fountain Plaza began to incur start-up costs.

With apartments, Larry had to pay a manager and maintenance personnel. With an inclusive retirement home, this expanded to salaries for kitchen staff, care providers, office personnel, and advertising. As Larry summarized for Ann: "The building is losing more than a hundred thousand a month! Bob Youngs was born an optimist. He projected a fillrate of ten occupants per month with forty on hand at opening and a break-even at seventy-percent. We're getting three quarters that fill, and break even looks closer to eighty-percent. It won't be long before we're back to Fountain Plaza owing us a million dollars."

"Should we cut costs until it fills?" Ann asked.

"Make more money than you spend and spend less money than you make. It's always better to make more money." Larry sighed and repeated. "Always better to make more money." He shook his head once. "Before this we took a lot of steps forward. Now this is a step backwards. But it's a small step." Larry got up to pace. An idea struck him. "Remember when you used to do television commercials for Lawrence's?"

"Well, yes. It wasn't as much fun as it sounds," Ann said.

Larry and Ann became the stars of several television commercials for Fountain Plaza. They talked to all of their friends and colleagues who had parents that were looking for an upscale retirement experience. Even their mothers, Elsie and Retta, moved into Fountain Plaza. At the monthly meeting with facility management, Larry and Ann received news that their television and word of mouth advertising had worked. By January the cash deficit had fallen to $75,000 and by February it was down to $50,000.

"At this rate, we might…might…be cashflow positive in July," Larry said.

"You mean get our money back?" Ann asked.

"Well, no." Larry scratched at the now familiar itch on the back of his neck. "I mean we won't have to loan anything else."

"That's something," Ann said.

Larry shook his head. "We'll be past a million and a quarter by then. I don't know where we'll get the credit."

"What are the Youngs putting up?" Ann asked.

"Nothing."

"Nothing?"

"They brought me on for financial backing," Larry said.

"That they're fifty-percent partners without taking on any risk doesn't seem right," Ann said. "Didn't they already get paid for their work as developers?"

Larry finally stopped scratching at his neck. "You know, you're right. Bob and his son have been paid for their work. If they want half the profit, they should assume half the risk. I could co-sign on a loan. We're nearly cashflow positive. There's no way the bank could say no."

Convincing the Youngs proved more difficult.

"You're the finance guy," Bob Youngs said.

"Well, yes. I secured the finances for construction and long-term. But this is start-up capital we're dealing with," Larry said.

"Why didn't you arrange for that?" Bob asked.

"You said it would start with an occupancy of forty and have a gain of ten per month. I financed for that. Costs just aren't lining up with projections. The bank is getting worried that I'm taking on too much debt against my stake in the enterprise."

"The deal was fifty-percent ownership," Bob said.

"I'm not asking to change that," Larry said, "I just want you to take out a loan against your stake in the business. The same amount I'm taking out. That's fifty-percent."

After the loan signing, Larry and Bob met at the bank to exchange funds in order to make the risk participation equal in Fountain Plaza.

"What's this ten-thousand dollar discrepancy? You didn't get a loan for the full amount," Larry said.

Bob Youngs shrugged.

"We should do something about this," Larry said.

"I just took out a six-hundred thousand dollar loan," Bob said.

"What if we remove the non-compete clause from our partnership agreement in exchange for not paying that difference?" Larry asked. The non-compete clause kept Larry from investing in any businesses that might infringe on Fountain Plaza's profitability. Larry knew one thing—constraints reduced his ability to act on opportunity.

"I suppose we could do that," Bob said.

"It's a deal," Larry said.

They shook hands.

Larry and Ann frequented Fountain Plaza for meals and to keep a close eye on their new property. It was during one such visit that Larry noticed: "Where's the piano we bought at the Crater Lake auction?"

"Wasn't Bob keeping it at his house during construction?" Ann asked.

Larry gave Bob a call.

"The piano?" Bob sounded confused on the line.

"Yes, the piano we bought for Fountain Plaza."

"What kind of a piano was it?"

"A grand piano," Larry said.

"You know, we sold that," Bob said.

"It wasn't yours to sell!"

"It was just sitting in our garage, taking up space. We had a rummage sale. We sold it."

"For how much?"

"Five-hundred dollars."

Larry sighed. He had paid more than that to buy it at auction to begin with. "Where's the money? You can write us a check."

"I don't have that kind of money right now," Bob said.

"We'll handle this with bookkeeping then," Larry said.

Larry worried the piano was just the start of the problem.

31

We'll See You in Court
Medford 1993

Fountain Plaza became cashflow-positive in September. Due to depreciation and other tax breaks, it had already been profitable, but now the property was putting money into Larry's accounts. "The dividends are tremendous," he told Ann. "With this cashflow, we have untapped borrowing."

When Larry looked at his assets, he saw more potential. Between rents from his apartments and dividends from the retirement home, his cashflow and borrowing power was growing by the month.

"We should build another retirement home," Larry said.

"Do you have a site in mind?" Ann asked.

Larry just smiled and took Ann to his Spring Street office. He swept his arm across the vacant lot adjacent to the Julia Ann apartments. "We already have the one lot." He pointed to several mounds of dirt. When leveling the ground for the Julia Ann and the Northwood apartments, they had used the lot to store excess dirt to avoid paying to have it hauled away. Larry pointed to the two adjoining lots. "I just bought the next two we need."

"Yokum finally sold?" Ann was startled. Larry had been in negotiations with him for 16 years.

"He wants to move into a retirement home. One-hundred and sixty-thousand got me both lots. Once we get the lot re-zoned, we'll be able to start another retirement home. We have enough cashflow we won't need partners this time." The Chief Tyee apartments had shown Larry how to do low-income housing, which he replicated with the Julia Ann apartments. So too, had Fountain Plaza shown him how to build a retirement community. Just as the Julia Ann apartments were the pinnacle of his apartment investments, so too could he leverage the lessons of Fountain Plaza to invest in a grand retirement home at the site adjacent to the Julia Ann apartments.

After the initial meeting at City Council to propose the zone change for more senior housing, Bob Youngs stormed into Larry's office. In one hand, Bob held a crumpled sheaf of papers.

"I hear about this from City Council? We have a non-compete clause in the contract." Bob shook the crumpled papers at Larry.

"We bought that out at the bank," Larry said.

"We did no such thing!"

"You were ten-thousand short. We took the clause off the books in exchange," Larry said.

"Then what's this—I got a note about owing you more money?" Bob unrolled the papers and held the wrinkled sheet up for Larry's inspection.

"For the piano."

Bob re-rolled the paper and hit it against his open palm.

"I never signed an agreement to let you out of the no-compete clause."

"It was a verbal agreement. It's right here in the minutes." Larry went to his filing cabinet and pulled up notes from their meeting at the Bank. "In exchange for forgiving ten thousand in debt, the non-compete clause has been removed from the partnership agreement."

"Until I see a signed contract, you have to stop working on this new retirement home."

"Fountain Plaza is already cashflow positive," Larry said. "There won't be any loss of business. Should we write up a contract for the non-compete right now? We can pay more money if that's what you need."

"You go through with this project and we'll sue," Bob said. He didn't bother to shake Larry's hand as he stomped out.

Craig, whose office was down the hall, peeked his head in. "I heard yelling. Everything all right?"

"The Youngs don't want us to build a new retirement home."

"What are you going to do?" Craig asked.

"I'm going to build it anyway."

"You're not worried that he's going to sue?"

"I'll find a way around it." Larry waved his hand dismissively. "Most importantly, there's a need for more retirement housing. If I don't fill it, someone else will."

Already Larry had land, an idea, and a name: Horton Plaza. A business search revealed there already was a Horton Plaza in San Diego, California, but none in Oregon. They could use the name, now all they needed was a design. Larry and Ann didn't want their new retirement home to be a copy of Fountain Plaza, so they went to San Diego seeking inspiration from the famous shopping center. Ultimately, they found little overlap between retail space and retirement housing. Continuing to search for something new, Ann and Larry returned to Portland to visit recently completed retirement homes. However, that didn't give them the unique look they sought, and ultimately Ann relied on her passion for a famous architect's work to lend style to the building:

"I'd really like to do something Frank Lloyd Wright inspired," Ann said. "The way he blends nature and buildings." Frank Lloyd Wright was known for putting straight modern lines in juxtaposition with the curves and bends of nature. The idea led to an open courtyard in the center of Horton Plaza, where koi ponds, trees, and curving walk-paths inserted a natural refuge.

"We can continue the theme inside," Ann said. "Something marvelous and natural in the lobby—and we can decorate the place with all those paintings I've been collecting from the Zonta auctions." She had acquired dozens of paintings from local artists. "Larry? Did you hear?"

"Paintings, yes." Larry pushed an egg around on his breakfast plate.

"You seem distracted. What's wrong?" Ann asked.

"It's this non-compete clause," Larry said.

"There's no way around it?"

Larry shook his head once: no.

"That's a shame. We really have some good ideas for the place. And the Youngs did agree to take the clause off at the bank." Ann sighed. "It would be such a nice legacy for our children and grandchildren."

Larry's eyes went wide open. "That's it!" He grabbed

his keys and bolted for the door.

"You haven't finished your breakfast!"

"No time!" The door closed behind him.

Within minutes he was at his office on Spring Street, engrossed in the contract for Fountain Plaza. He obsessed over the non-compete clause: "No partner shall participate more than 10% in a competing enterprise..." Larry began to pace.

By the time Craig reached the office, Larry already had the plan in mind: "We include the grandkids as partners."

"What?" Craig asked.

"Ann and I keep ten percent. The other ninety is split ten ways. Ann and I can retain control. But only at ten percent."

"I guess that might work," Craig said.

"Of course it will work. It's in the contract. There's no way they can sue," Larry hurried back to his office. "Do you think the lawyer has started working yet today? It doesn't matter. I'll leave a message."

After organizing the project into a partnership with the grandchildren, Larry began gathering construction funding. HUD allowed additional loans on projects that were at least 20 years old. Both Julia Ann Apartments and Chief Tyree Apartments met that requirement. Larry took out second mortgages on each of them at 8.25% with a 40-year term.

Construction began on Horton Plaza. Dirt was trucked off the site and the land was flattened. After the foundation went in, Larry received bad news. He broke it to Ann: "I thought I found a way around the Youngs—they sued us anyway."

"What are they asking for?" Ann asked.

"Two and a half million dollars." He held up the lawsuit documents. There were a lot of them.

Ann balked. "Two and a half million?"

Larry nodded.

"On what grounds?"

"Non-compete, breach of contract, excessive compensation...there's something in there about sixty thousand for drawings he had done on a similar project—of course there's no provision in the partnership agreement for any such payment." Larry sighed.

"I suppose we should get a lawyer," Ann said.

"Why not two. One for each of us?"

They hired Kellerman and Stout, two lawyers from different practices so as to gain access to as much legal expertise as possible. Kellerman was a younger man, and Stout more seasoned. They were both specialists in business and real estate law with focuses in litigation. When Ann and Larry met with them, they all shook hands and Larry got straight to business: "Do they have any merit for this lawsuit?"

"Well. Yes and no," Kellerman said. "They have enough of a case that a judge won't throw it out as being frivolous. So we conduct discovery and see if there's any real merit."

"How does discovery work?" Ann asked.

"We'll start by subpoenaing relevant documents and requesting interrogatories. Based on that, we'll conduct depositions."

"Depositions, you mean answer questions under oath?" Ann asked.

"Don't worry about them. Just tell the truth...you'll probably have to pay something, but not the whole two and a half million," Kellerman said.

"Why should we have to pay?" Larry asked.

"We'll get to that. But first, I have a more important question: are your assets protected?" Stout asked.

"The apartments are each LLCs. So is Fountain Plaza. They're all individual entities. So we're protected from liability," Larry said.

"Protected from outside liability. Because of your partnership, the Youngs are suing you directly," Kellerman said.

"They can go after the assets you own," Stout said. "They can go after your ownership in these LLCs."

Larry felt sick to his stomach. A glance at Ann and he knew she felt as ill at the thought. Larry had been building a housing empire for the last several decades. It hadn't been a get rich fast plan, but a plan of steady reliable growth. Now, that which was to be his greatest achievement—Horton Plaza—threatened all of his investments. Making things worse, this wasn't a matter Larry could resolve with a phone call or by lobbying City Hall.

"What can we do?" Larry asked.

"Between the two of us, we'll figure something out," Stout nodded to Kellerman.

A few months later, Ann and Larry were called for their first round of depositions at the offices of the Youngs's lawyers. All interested parties were present. Sitting across the table from Bob Youngs tested Larry's patience. He would have preferred to simply work out a deal. All this legal due process aggravated the itch that was spreading across Larry's body.

Kellerman swore Bob Youngs in first. "Remember,

you're under oath, and only able to answer questions, not ask them. Also, since you're under oath, things you say are admissible in both criminal and civil court."

"I understand," Bob said.

Kellerman and Stout proceeded to ask questions, leading to the reveal of fifty-eight fabrications, omissions, and other corrections to the initial lawsuit.

Afterwards, Larry and Ann debriefed with Kellerman and Stout.

"I talked with their lawyers," Stout said, "they're dropping counsel."

"So we won?" Larry asked.

"No. It means we have to do this all over again—different lawyers and a more accurate lawsuit," Stout said.

32

Horton Plaza
Medford 1995

Construction of Horton Plaza continued while the Youngs pressed litigation. Any mail addressed from a law office, or in any way hinting of legality, agitated a burst of anxiety in Larry. Still, he had made his decision, and until someone forced him to stop, he'd do everything to accomplish his vision for Horton Plaza—the perfect balance of upscale retirement living and affordability. Litigation and construction continued in parallel until Horton Plaza's ribbon cutting ceremony in May of 1995. Larry had the honor of using the oversized shears. Afterward, he and Ann walked the halls of the new building.

"The paintings really liven up the place," Larry said. Just as planned, Ann's collection of paintings from local artists were some of the first decorations to be installed.

"I'm glad we found use for them," Ann said.

"You know, my offices are right here in the building now," Larry said. Medford Better Housing had moved from a trailer on the lot, to the Northwest corner of Horton Plaza to become the first tenants of the building.

"It would be a real short commute to live here."

Ann laughed. "I'm not ready for a retirement home."

"I'm moving to Horton Plaza." Some part of him wanted to experience the upscale retirement lifestyle now —in case the lawsuit turned for the worse and he lost the property. He stood still in the hall and smiled at her. "If you want to live with me, you'll live here too."

"Oh Larry, be serious," Ann said. She waited for Larry's smile to turn impish, sly, or coy, anything other than genuine. But the smile didn't shift. "You are being serious." Ann tried to think of a reason why not to live in a retirement home but the truth was she had always felt a little unsafe at their Barneburg house after the break-in. She sighed. "Only if I can have a nice bathroom and a big kitchen."

"Done!"

Ann got both but only cooked three meals over the next twenty years. The food in the dining hall was simply too good and too convenient.

Among the other lessons learned from Fountain Plaza was that occupancy needed to be addressed early. By aggressively pre-filling units for this new retirement home, including signing up both Larry and Ann's mothers, they were able to make the home profitable much faster than Fountain Plaza.

Larry's mother, Retta, made the move to Horton Plaza as one of the first residents. She told Larry, "I'm proud that I've lived in all of your housing projects." She died later that same year on September 20th, 1995. It was a difficult loss for Larry. His mother's insistence on education had started the spark of continued self-improvement that led to his being the first college graduate in his family and ultimately to his passion for investing. Without that initial push from his mother, he might have remained a low-income wage earner. Instead, he lived a blessed life.

Larry had continued to champion education with the decision several years prior to send each of his boys through college if he could. Three of them attended the University or Oregon, with Craig earning a degree in Business, Stan earning a degree in Journalism, and Steve dropping out due to illness. Chuck graduated from Larry's alma mater, Oregon State University with a degree in Teaching. Instead of college, Jerry chose to become a goldsmith, and attended trade school before going to work at Lawrence's Jewelers.

Several years, and several sets of Youngs's attorneys later, it was 1998. Larry and Ann had accrued over one-hundred thousand in legal fees. Worse than that, Larry hadn't begun any new investment projects even though his financial statement showed room to borrow—still, he felt paralyzed by the now four year old lawsuit. He needed to keep capital available in case things turned for the worse and his property empire was put in jeopardy.

"We have a breakthrough," Kellerman told Ann and Larry. "The Youngs have agreed to a buy out. With mediation, we can be done by year's end."

The first step was to have Fountain Plaza appraised. In spite of the State of Oregon's 9% loan, the net value of Fountain Plaza was $4 Million. With that value in hand, the partners met with a mediator.

"We want two mil. That's half. That's fair," Bob Youngs said.

By the end of the first mediation, Larry's itch had migrated to his legs and broke out in shingles.

Larry needed help. He met with Craig.

"I don't know if we're going to be able to reach a settlement with the Youngs. They just want so much," Larry said.

"You can go to two million," Craig said.

"Where's the money going to come from!?" Larry scratched his leg.

"You were able to borrow a million and a quarter for construction and startup," Craig reminded him.

"Horton Plaza ate a lot of that credit," Larry said. "I've got a half million in savings. Maybe…maybe I can do one point seven mil."

"Is that going to be enough?" Craig asked.

"It'll have to be—but I think I have an idea," Larry said.

Mediation continued.

"I can't finance two million," Larry told the Youngs. "We can have a judge put the property up for sale. Then we can split any profit from that."

The look on Bob Youngs face was one of shock and fear. "The loan's not re-financable. Nobody's going to pay four mil on top of that…we still have that loan against start-up capital. We can barely make interest payments on it. If it sells too low at auction, we could be underwater!"

Larry had already paid back his start-up loans. What he couldn't pay off early, was the 9% loan to the State of Oregon. Monthly payments were around $50,000. Those payments ate a substantial chunk out of what the building would otherwise provide as dividends. Unfortunately, there was no way to reduce or eliminate those payments until the loan completed its term in 2021. That was 25 years away.

Larry made his gamble, "Then I can give you one million, seven-hundred thousand."

Bob thought it over. He nodded several times. "I could go as low as a mil-eight."

It was a deal. Larry agreed to pay the Youngs $1.8 Million in 90 days. Larry would end up with full ownership of Fountain Plaza and its 9% 30-year State of Oregon loan.

Larry continued to meet with Craig to find clever financing solutions.

"I can borrow against the Valley of the Rogue Bank stock that I put in the kid's names," Larry said.

"Taking a loan against bank stock. That's kind of risky," Craig said. "What if they want to sell the stock to keep margin? We wouldn't have any say."

"Horton Plaza will be paying me back for money loaned and the apartments are making a lot of cashflow," Larry countered. "We'll pay it back. We just need to come up with the money for the settlement."

After tapping every available line of credit, they were still $60,000 short with two weeks left to close the settlement. Larry checked the books for Fountain Plaza. Between the dividend that was ready for dispersal and the money put aside for the upcoming loan payment, there was enough to cover the last gap. Larry used Fountain Plaza's own funds to finish the buyout of the Youngs. Every dollar his other properties produced went to putting money back into Fountain Plaza's account by the end of the month when the State of Oregon did a routine audit. It was a risky maneuver, but he paid the money back with one day to spare. By then, Larry felt he would die from the itch of shingles.

But he found the money. Fountain Plaza was his and Horton Plaza could continue to build a legacy to pass on to his family.

33

Retirement
Medford 1998

In 1993, an earthquake struck Klamath Falls, Oregon, causing over ten million dollars in property damage. Communities in Oregon began performing studies on the earthquake survivability of the older buildings in the state. It was in late 1998 that Medford's survey of downtown revealed the building housing Lawrence's Jewelers was beginning to collapse. Several bricks had deteriorated and crumbled in the East wall of the building.

The city of Medford condemned the building, reducing its value to one-hundred and ten thousand dollars.

A representative of the Medford Seismic Council met with Ann and Bob to discuss the building. They had to bring the building up to seismic code or it would be demolished. Initial estimates on repairs came in at one million dollars. With Larry's help, they lined up a remodeling loan for the building.

Bob reviewed the final loan papers at his repair bench. He put them to the side and stared at the seat next to his bench where Elsie had sat to talk to customers. Three years prior, she had fallen, broken her hip, and caught pneumonia while in the hospital. She died two weeks later on January 25th, 1995. Her funeral had been standing room only at the Episcopal church. The loss of Elsie had been a major blow to Lawrence's Jewelers.

When Ann saw that Bob was staring at Elsie's old chair, she went over to talk to him.

"What's on your mind?" Ann asked.

Bob looked up with a sober expression. "Times are changing. The mall is taking all the gravy out of downtown," Bob said. "Now we're becoming like any other store. We lost the base. Our customers are dying off. Kids have moved away. The new customers don't have the same history. It's an entirely new situation."

"We'll keep earning new customers," Ann said.

Bob resumed staring at Elsie's vacant seat. His eyes filled with emotion and he removed his glasses to wipe his eyes before tears could escape.

"We keep doing what mother did, treat people nicely, treat them as friends," Ann said.

Bob nodded. "Give them a good product at a good price." His words sounded hollow, lacking his normal chipper energy.

"About this building remodel. I could sign for it, but I don't know if I want to do that. It won't be paid off until I'm a hundred and fifteen. I figure I won't make it that far." He laughed, with morbid cheer. "I don't want my kids to have to worry about it."

Bob stood and placed his hands on the back of Elsie's empty chair. "I'm ready to retire."

While Bob had put some money away for retirement, his two largest investments were the store and the building it resided in. Ann liquidated most of her retirement account to buyout Bob's stake in the business through a lump sum and monthly payments. Shares in the building, however, were greatly devalued due to the looming million dollar renovation. Both Bob and Ann sold their stake in the building to Jerry and Chuck at a deep discount. Even with that low cost of acquisition, the payments on a million dollar loan were more than the jewelry store would be able to afford. Larry and Ann gladly donated a million dollars to preserve the historic downtown building.

Construction began. Lawrence's Jewelers remained open during remodel. The first phase was to tear down the front of the building where the brick had been crumbling. The source of the problem was revealed to be a rusted out drainpipe from the upper corner of the neighboring building. With every heavy rain, a little more mortar would wash out, and water would leak into Lawrence's Jewelers, resulting in a difficult to eradicate musty smell. With every freeze, the trapped water deteriorated a few more bricks. Both buildings had been a ticking time bomb towards collapse. Fortunately the damage was found in time, and both buildings could be saved.

It wasn't much past Bob's retirement that Ann was in her seventies. The strain of standing all day to clerk at the store began to take its toll on her hips. Eventually, she had to admit that much as her mother had once told her, "It is better to wear out than to rust out." And wearing out she was. It was with a heavy heart that she told Jerry, "I've really enjoyed working at the store. Bob has retired. Now it is time for me to retire as well. I'll still be able to advise you on running the business, and I can do appraisals on gemstones. But the day-to-day business is going to be yours now."

Jerry took over the store. It was easy for him to stay on, especially since he had remarried April 8th 1995 to Jodi Matchett, and now he and his wife were raising a toddler —Ann and Larry's 11th grandchild.

34

The World Calls
Machu Pichu 2003

Sprawling stone terraces capped the mountain. Grass grew wild on the terraced gardens, stretching a verdant blanket between the sun-bleached stone foundations. Glacial valleys and rugged mountain peaks stretched in every direction. Standing on Machu Pichu was like standing on top of the world.

"It's so much bigger than I could have possibly imagined," Ann said. "It's just huge." It boggled her mind that man could make something so vast in such a remote location. Ann would forever remember it as one of the highlights of her global travel.

Where Machu Pichu roused, India disheartened. Ann befriended one of their tour guides, an attorney at law. Because she was a woman, she was unable to make a living as a lawyer and had to work a second job as a tour guide. "My husband's mother controls the family," the woman said. "She decides what we are to do. It was a struggle to convince her to let me study law."

That, coupled with the incredible poverty in India broke Ann's heart. It was difficult for her to watch so many people reduced to begging.

Taiwan gave them a different look at relative poverty.

For one of their meals, they had Peking Duck. By the time they had stopped to eat, Ann and Larry were both starving. The waiters brought out crispy Mandarin pancakes, white scallions, and plumb sauce. Without realizing they were supposed to wait for the duck, Ann and Larry ate the pancakes and scallions.

When the waiter brought out the whole duck, he clucked in laughter at the tourists who had eaten all the pancakes early. Between the two of them, they ate half of the duck. They brought the rest to the hotel to share with the people working there.

In the next morning, the staff came down to see who had shared the duck. Peking duck was one of the most expensive and difficult to prepare culinary dishes. Giving it away was similar to sharing a feast.

Ann and Larry's trips around the world took them to Paris where no amount of time seemed sufficient to see the Louvre in its entirety. They went to Italy: Pompeii, Florence, and Rome. At the latter, they lunched outside while workers unearthed Roman ruins in the middle of the street. Likely the ruins were discovered while attempting to put in new metro lines.

They took an Oregon State Alumni tour through the Vatican. It was a private tour that took them into areas normally off limits to the public. The highlight of the tour was a private visit to the Sistine Chapel. No crowds. No noise. Just a moment to look up and reflect on Michelangelo's masterpiece.

Outside, they saw the changing of the Swiss Guard in their colorful orange, blue, and red-striped uniforms.

Likewise in England, they saw the changing of the guard and were able to wave at the Queen as her motorcade took her from Buckingham Palace to an event of state.

In New York they saw Broadway on a shoestring. Eight plays in five days. In England, it was Kabuki Theater.

Cairo proved to have its own challenges.

"You're not getting me on an elephant." Ann shook her head. They had to take a jeep. It bounced across the sandy desert towards the distant looming pyramids.

"The elephant would have been smoother," Larry quipped.

The Gemological Institute of America, commonly known as the GIA, celebrated its 75th anniversary in Carlsbad, California, in 2006. Ann held multiple certifications with the GIA, and convinced Larry to accompany her to the celebration. There was plenty of entertainment. A local outdoor pool featured synchronized swimmers. The Museum of Making Music created an industrial sized harp for the event by hanging strings between the building and the lawn. Street performers abounded, including a living statue with plaster moulds.

Madeline Albright, the keynote speaker, encouraged the crowd, "It is no surprise to this audience that gems and jewelry can be used as forms of communication."

After her speech, there were fireworks and the largest charcuterie table Ann and Larry had ever seen, overflowing with exotic breads, meats and cheeses.

"This is the biggest, most wonderful party I've ever been to," Ann told Larry.

"Even better than the trade shows?" Larry asked.

"Those were fun, this is something special," she said.

They saw gems from around the world and were educated on the upcoming movie *Blood Diamonds*. Ann came away from the presentations on blood diamonds with her head reeling.

"At least the jewelry industry is working to fix the problem," Ann said.

"They can't do that overnight," Larry said.

"No, but new technology is making it easier to track a diamond's origin by analyzing the inner materials. They can block blood diamonds from distribution." The largest importer of diamonds, the United States, did just that.

Even though Ann considered herself retired from the jewelry business, she still attended the annual Tucson, Arizona gem show. Larry, who had run out of genealogical leads, needed something to entertain him while she attended the event. He handed Ann a brochure.

"We can stay at a ranch," he said.

"A ranch?"

"White Stallion Ranch…they have cabins, serve meals, and offer two horse rides a day."

"Why not?" Ann agreed.

They arrived in the evening. Larry wore ostentatious red boots and a stylish black hat. As they walked the ranch grounds, Larry noticed he was getting an unusual number of stares.

"Nice hat," someone said.

"Nice boots," another said.

Larry whispered to Ann, "I thought we were supposed to dress like cowboys."

"Maybe you over-did it?" Ann suggested.

Another guest of the ranch asked, "Are you part of the program?"

"The program?" Larry was confused—until a man wearing similar red boots and black hat stepped in front of the bonfire with a guitar and began to sing.

White Stallion Ranch featured nightly entertainment, including astronomy shows, line dancing lessons, nature and animal programs, and Loop Rawlins's Wild West Show of Trick Roping. Loop, a Tucson native, went on to perform with Cirque du Soleil, and was a quarterfinalist on America's Got Talent.

However, the primary reason Larry chose the ranch was for the horseback rides. After several days of gentle rides, Larry suggested, "Let's go on a mountain ride."

"Why not?" Ann agreed.

The trail they took was rutted into gullies in several places. Rain made rocks shiny and wet, and the soil muddy and intractable. During an ascent, Ann felt her horse slip and fall...straight down. Ann gripped the sides of the saddle with her thighs, her fingers white knuckled on the reins. Thump. Ann's boots were on the muddy ground on either side of the horse.

"What happened?" Larry asked.

"My horse collapsed." Ann couldn't get leverage to slide off the horse.

"Where are its legs?" Larry asked.

Ann peered around the flank of the horse. Somehow, its legs had folded up under it inside a gully. The horse's body seemed wedged in the tight space.

"Can you get the trail boss?" Ann asked.

"Yes, yes, I can do that," Larry said.

His horse clopped off through the mud. Ann's horse

apparently decided to follow, and rose up. Ann's grip had gone soft while straddling the horse in the mud, and the sudden action of the horse rising to its feet was enough to knock Ann over backwards off the saddle. She cried out and fell backwards. Her head hit first. On a rock.

Her vision wavered in and out, going slowly darker. She heard Larry's voice. It sounded like he was in a tunnel. "That's a lot of blood."

"You're not helping, dear," Ann said. Larry eased her to a sitting position. Some vision returned. She felt the back of her head...wet. She was afraid to look. Hopefully it would just be water...nope, blood. A lot of blood. Larry had been right.

"Head wounds," Ann said absently.

The trail boss called back to the ranch for someone to come get Ann. They kept pressure on the wound as they took her to urgent care. Several stitches and plenty of fluids later, Ann was discharged.

"At least they didn't have to shave a bald spot," Ann said.

Larry, however, grinned ear to ear. "I negotiated with the ranch. They agreed to give us a discount of ten percent off the next year."

"I hit my head and you were negotiating?" Ann asked.

"It's a good deal," Larry said.

"I could have died," Ann said.

"You were fine." Larry's relaxed tone put Ann at ease. "So you'll come back?" he asked.

"As long as I get a better horse next time," Ann said.

They laughed away the last of the tension from the event. They didn't just return the next year, but every year for the next decade. White Stallion Ranch became their favorite vacation destination.

During the last of their trips, Tucson froze, with the temperature dropping twenty degrees below zero. The residents of Tucson were unused to the cold, and one stranger offered to buy Ann's faux-fur lined winter coat.

"It's not for sale, but thank you." Ann's breath puffed as she said it.

At the gem show, Ann bought both for Lawrence's as well as private customers with special orders, such as one customer who had lost an amethyst from her ring and wanted an exact match to the remaining amethysts. Getting a match like that from traveling vendors would be impossible, as would getting an exact match from a catalogue. But, at a gem show, there were vendors from all over the region, offering thousands of options.

Ann found one display case that had hundreds of tiny amethysts that appeared the exact shade of violet that she sought.

"Can I see that tray?" Ann asked.

"Of course." The vendor pulled the tray from the case, catching a corner in the process, causing the entire tray to upend. Hundreds of tiny violet amethysts scattered across the floor.

"Oh dear," Ann muttered.

Eventually the stones were recovered, and Ann found her customer's match. On her way out of the show that day, she stopped near a drawing outside a garden display. Ann crumpled a business card and added it to the drawing basket.

Two months later, she received a call.

"It's the Tucson Gift Show. Congratulations, you won a trip to Buchart Gardens and a night stay in Vancouver,

British Columbia." The same place that Ann had gone on honeymoon with Chuck Sr. It was a memory from the past that Ann had nearly forgotten. Still, she buried those memories and told Larry of the stroke of luck.

Larry's response wasn't what Ann expected: "Since we're in Vancouver, let's coincide that with a cruise to Alaska. We can take a train from Anchorage to Fairbanks, stay overnight at Denali—it'll only cost six thousand more."

Ann laughed and readily agreed.

35

Closing the Store
Medford 2007

While managing Lawrence's II in the mall, Chuck's blood pressure was nearing 200/120—a level considered a hypertension emergency. The business which had flourished for much of the late nineties and early two-thousands was now struggling to maintain profitability. Chuck decided to retire and close the mall store. In April of 2008, he remarried to Joanna "Asia" Kubiak, a Polish immigrant. A few years of diet changes, exercise, and a reduction of stress restored his blood pressure to healthy levels.

While Larry and Ann didn't fully recoup their investment in Lawrence's II, their losses were minimal and their investment had created a business that employed dozens of people in the Rogue Valley. The close of the mall store gave the downtown location a brief lift in business.

The summer of 2008, Lawrence's Jewelers hosted a centennial celebration in downtown Medford. The celebration was a success, with hundreds in attendance, including family from around the region. For the event, they closed a block of Bartlett Street. There was live music, a catered dinner, and free copies of *Always Do the Right Thing: The One Hundred Year Legacy of Lawrence's Jewelers,* by Dawna Curler.

Ann was so busy greeting people and thanking lifelong customers that by the time she sat down to eat, her dinner had gone cold. Still, the quality was there.

"The food is great," Ann said.

"David really out did himself," Larry said. The chef they hired for the evening had the distinction of previously working as a chef at Donald Trump's Mar-a-lago Estate in Florida.

Unfortunately, changing shopping habits continued to whittle at the store's bottom line.

"How's business looking?" Ann asked Jerry.

"Well, we have a store room full of a hundred years of outdated merchandise. We're using ebay to get rid of that and make room for some updated fine china and everyday china." He shook his head once. "I don't know if it'll be enough. Downtown isn't the thriving shopping area it once was. The bridal registry disappeared for us—people don't want fine china or crystal anymore, they want towels and kitchen appliances. So now they go to Target," Jerry said. Target had other advantages too, such as a bridal registry that could be accessed around the globe. It was becoming increasingly difficult for a small, family run business to compete.

Over the next decade, more big box shopping centers emerged in Medford: Best Buy, Sportsman's Warehouse, WalMart, Target, Costco. Soon, Medford's shopping was indistinguishable from Southern California.

More worrisome to Ann than the business's profitability: "How's your health holding up?"

Much the way that the stress of operating Lawrence's II in the mall had been straining Chuck's health, Jerry too was having deteriorating health. It was a major blow to Jerry, who had ridden his bicycle to work more often than he drove—when they had Lawrence's III in Ashland, Jerry rode the twenty-five miles from Eagle Point to Ashland there and back every day. His dedication to cycling was driven by his passion for competitive off-road mountain bike racing. That dedication and passion had been enough to earn him a National Championship in 2000. Now, however, he was diagnosed as pre-diabetic. The medicine they used to treat his disorder came with complications leading to blood pressure issues. He needed to retire and save his health the same that Chuck had done years earlier. Ultimately, the discovery of several food allergies led to an improvement in Jerry's health.

When Lawrence's closed its doors in 2015, Ann inherited thousands of leftover pinecones. Many were the same ones that her father had gathered at Diamond Lake over the years. She recalled how he would toast the pinecones so that they would open and release their seeds. Then he would take the seeds back to Diamond Lake and spread them around for the squirrels. It was a good memory. She looked around the now closed Lawrence's Jewelers. The store had given her a purpose when her first marriage ended by death and her second by betrayal. It had accompanied her through her marriage to Larry. Ultimately five generations of family had worked there, from Ann's grandfather to three of her grandsons.

36

Building A Future
Medford 1999

Four years had passed since Horton Plaza's opening. The building was near full capacity and Larry felt that Medford was ready for another upscale retirement home. While he was seeing dividends from Fountain Plaza, his attempt to sidestep the Youngs's litigation had caused his investment in Horton Plaza to primarily come from money loaned to the retirement home. While he was receiving substantial loan payments, he wasn't gaining the equity needed to secure more credit. In order to build another retirement home, he'd need to take on another partner.

Larry decided to take out an advertisement in the Medford Mail Tribune asking for partners to develop a new retirement home in Medford. He only received one call from Mike and Mary Mahar. The Mahars were well known and well respected developers in the Rogue Valley. Checking references was easy. Practically anyone he asked had something good to say about the Mahars.

Larry and Mike met at the location that would become Anna Maria Creekside. "I can't put up enough equity on my own to get a loan," Larry explained. "The project will make money, but I need more equity."

Mike agreed to the project. They shook hands and started developing an LLC so one person could be the decision maker while other interested parties would simply draw dividends. This business structure became the preferred organization for Larry's business investments.

Shortly after starting construction on Anna Maria, Larry had an unexpected visit from Bill Terpening.

"I can't find a buyer for my land. I'll sell it to you for six-hundred thousand," Bill said. The first time Bill had offered to sell his family land in Eugene, the appraisal had been $800,000. "We can make a retirement home. Let's call it Terpening Terrace."

The two-hundred thousand dollar price-cut was enough to get Larry interested in the project. Had Bill come to Larry a few months earlier, it would have been a done deal. Anna Maria, however, tied up significant financial resources—and he'd already had to take on a partner for that project.

Larry created a three-year forecast for his cashflow so he could determine how large of a loan payment he could afford and calculate how much cash he needed to keep on hand. Combining the two values gave him the amount he could invest in the property.

He talked it over with Ann.

"It's a good opportunity," Larry said. "We'll have to rely on other partners, but the returns will be worth it. A small part of a money making endeavor is better than the whole part of a non-money making endeavor. What good is identifying opportunities if you don't take advantage of them?" Their final stake in Terpening Terrace was 15%.

It became a race between Anna Maria and Terpening Terrace to see which building would be completed first. Both projects encountered construction delays and cost overruns.

The site for Anna Maria was filled with soil taken from a nearby golf course, which left the ground too mushy and prone to settling for a large building. A concrete foundation would have put them well over cost. Fortunately, they found a solution: a slurry of ash and cement that lowered the cost and yielded stable ground for construction.

For Terpening Terrace, Eugene limited the surface parking, requiring the construction of parking garages. Since the area was a flood zone, they had to bring in dirt to raise the land, which killed trees and incurred city fines. Larry hired a lawyer and an arborist who argued that the trees had been planted by the Terpenings and were not indigenous—reducing the city fines.

With both projects back on track, Larry and Ann had an opportunity to travel for a different sort of milestone. Larry's second son, Stan, was celebrating his fiftieth birthday in Las Vegas. The day before his birthday, on July 8th, 1999, Larry and Stan began the day with a morning round of golf.

On their way back from the round of golf, rain started to fall. Back at the hotel, Ann and Larry watched the storm through a lobby window. Oregon saw a lot of rainfall, but it rarely had storms of this intensity.

"Look at it come down," Ann said.

The rain was a torrent. Stan approached, his head shaking back and forth.

"The show's canceled due to the flood," Stan said,

"The magician, Lance Burton, can't get here."

"Can you get tickets for tomorrow's show?" Ann asked.

"There won't be another show while we're in town," Stan said.

They watched as gold-brown floodwaters ran down the Las Vegas strip, submerging a few unlucky cars. Flood waters from the thunderstorms would go on to cause over twenty-million dollars in property damage.

Upon return to Medford, Ann and Larry were able to tour the now nearly complete Anna Maria facility. Y2K was on everyone's mind, and Larry had to shake off the thought that the Las Vegas flood was some ill-omen foreshadowing the end of the world. After all, he had been in Mexico during a deadly earthquake and the world kept turning. Still, it was difficult not to get sucked into the YK2 hype, which seemed to play often on the news. Nobody was sure just how severe the year 2000 bug would be for embedded software. The bug itself was that older computer software typically only stored the last two digits of a date. 1999 was stored as 99. When the computer rolled over to 00, the worry was that outdated software would think it was 1900. When 2000 came around, there were very few reported instances of issues. The world didn't end and everyone breathed a sigh of relief.

Terpening Terrace finished at nearly the same time as Anna Maria. As Bill Clinton's second term transitioned to George H. Bush's first term, the economy was on fire. Both buildings filled quickly and started generating excellent returns.

Then, on a Tuesday morning, Ann woke to the news. She always kept her radio set to music, yet an urgent voice roused her from sleep. "A twin-engine plane has flown into the World Trade Center. Witnesses report hearing a huge explosion—and heavy smoke can be seen billowing from the building."

Ann bolted upright in bed. Fearing a hoax, she changed the station on her radio. "At this point, we have no word on casualties." What Ann was hearing were the first AP news reports from the day that would become known as 9/11.

She hurried to wake Larry. The two of them settled in their chairs in the living room to watch Fox News's coverage of the event. They watched live as the second jetliner raced through the sky and collided in a furious explosion against the second World Trade Center tower.

While members of Larry's and Ann's family had served in World War II, the Korean War, and the Vietnam War, none of their grandchildren were part of the armed forces for this new war.

While the US war in Iraq and Afghanistan built momentum, Larry kept his focus on investments. Real estate proved to be relatively resistant to wartime impact.

With both Anna Maria and Terpening Terrace providing excellent dividends, Larry had considerable borrowing potential. Unfortunately, both Medford and Eugene were currently meeting the retirement demand. What he needed was a new community to invest in.

The architect Ron Grimes found a location in Bend, Oregon. The project was Whispering Winds. This time, when Larry crunched numbers, he knew he could take on a larger stake than the last retirement home and he and Ann offered to take 25% ownership in the project.

After construction, an issue of staffing arose. Ann and Larry were now owners of or partners in five retirement homes. Larry, at the age of 80, tried his hand at being General Manager for Fountain Plaza and Horton Plaza. The workload was more than the mostly-retired Larry wanted to take on. He couldn't just hire anyone—he needed a world class General Manager to keep operations running smoothly. Fortunately, he had a candidate in mind:

"Mary Roper," Larry told Ann.

"Who's that?"

"The manager at Eugene had worked with her before. She owns retirement communities in Tacoma and Port Angeles. She also runs Dharma Healthcare, Co. I looked into her. She's got a good record."

After Ann and Larry's first meeting with Mary, Ann blurted, "Oh my goodness, she's very smart."

"Well, she is an author," Larry added, "and her father is a legislator."

Mary started at Whispering Winds and soon was promoted to be General Manager for all of the Horton Properties retirement homes. To date there hasn't been a single dip in performance or even a hint of friction with any of her managers.

With management solved, Larry focused on investments. For his next project, he partnered with Doug Dense, who was already a partner in retirement homes in Roseburg and Eugene. They undertook Countryside Village in Grants Pass where Larry and Ann owned several acres of land that they had acquired from Ann's cousin.

Every time Larry looked at his assets, he saw more potential. The dividends from the retirement homes were increasing. His cashflow and borrowing power grew by the month.

"I can do better," he told Ann.

"How much do we need?" Ann asked.

"It isn't a matter of need, but one of potential," Larry said.

"You mean like Ayn Rand said, 'productive achievement as man's noblest activity?'"

Larry grinned. "Exactly like that."

37

What we Leave Behind
Portland 2004

Larry and Ann revised their estate plan for the third time under the guidance of Holland and Knight out of Portland. This allowed an opportunity to better secure the Horton Children's Trust against lawsuits and start the Horton Family Foundation, a charitable organization focused on works in the Rogue Valley.

With the help of an estate planner, they made updates. During one meeting, an estate lawyer asked Larry, "How much income do you want for the rest of your life? How much money a year?"

"As high as I can. I don't know what inflation is going to be like. What about three-hundred thousand a year?" At the time, Larry's real estate investments were bringing in over a million dollars per year.

"For tax reasons, I'd recommend two-hundred-fifty-thousand," the estate planner said. "You can put your assets in an estate in exchange for a note. You get payments. Give the rest back to your family. You'll save on taxes. Your estate will live on."

While Larry could have easily called it quits then, and

enjoyed the rest of his retirement, he couldn't forget his conversation with Ann. *Productive achievement is the noblest activity.*

Demand for Horton Plaza, Fountain Plaza, and Anna Maria was greater than the housing the three buildings could provide. From Larry's own rule of thumb, it had been more than four years since a retirement home opened in the community. It was time to invest.

With his growing knowledge of the retirement home business, he took on his most ambitious project yet: Veranda Park. Once again, he partnered with Mike Mahar. The vision for the facility was to make the most upscale retirement experience available in Southern Oregon. Mike took a large stake in the partnership, freeing up Larry's assets for another investment opportunity, which he took in Central Point. The facility was to be called Twin Creeks.

Veranda Park finished construction a few months before the housing bubble popped in 2007. Twin Creeks was already in construction. Both properties were forced to startup during a collapsing housing market. Most Americans relied upon their house as the primary investment towards retirement—Larry's retirement home model heavily relied on the sale of those lifelong investments to provide enough capital to provide for pleasant golden years. This economic downturn stagnated retirement home applications.

While Anna Maria and Terpening Terrace had raced to see which building would completed first, Veranda Park and Twin Creeks were embroiled in a different competition: which would be cashflow positive first.

Larry and the investors from Twin Creeks placed bets.

Larry picked Veranda Park. It was in the larger population area—Medford—and it was an older building already starting to fill. However, a conflux of falling home prices and upscale environment made Veranda Park sluggish in growth towards its potential. Twin Creeks filled first. It cost Larry dinner for six at Callahan's.

Things didn't improve for Veranda Park. Due to the heavy negative cashflow, Larry and Mike Mahar were forced to fund the struggling business.

"This is a really big check," Craig said as he reviewed the books.

"Failure isn't an option," Larry said. "Mike and I are trying to get the building refinanced. That will help."

"I don't think you're going to get your money back," Craig said.

"We have to stay focused. We made a decision, we'll stick to it," Larry said. "The odds are good that we can break even."

Before the buildings could be refinanced, an investment group made an offer to buy the buildings Larry had invested in with Mike Mahar—both Anna Maria and Veranda Park—in a joint sale. The final sale price: $50,000,000. That's fifty million. Larry used part of the sale to do a 1031 exchange to buy Horton Plaza from the Grandchildren's trust, making Horton Properties 100% owners of Horton Plaza, and giving the grandchildren their inheritance early. After all the loans for Anna Maria and Veranda Park were paid off, Larry took three million to the bank, with a third of that earmarked for taxes. To make the deal even sweeter, the dividend from Anna Maria had been around $29,000 per month, while the dividend from Horton Plaza was nearly $40,000 per month.

"I'll be darned, you did it," Craig said.

"Anything is possible. Once you have the vision and strategy, follow through on it." It had been a lifetime of self-improvement and making positive partnerships that benefited all parties. At every opportunity Larry had taken as big of a risk as he could. Every time the risk paid off he looked for a bigger risk. "Start with small risks. Find out what works. Then grow. Don't flinch. Keep focused on the goal. Everything will fall into place."

And it did. The total gross rents for all of the properties Larry owned now exceeded $10 Million annual, with a return of nearly $2 Million in annual dividends. The entire estate was placed under Horton Properties LLC to ensure that the housing empire that Larry created would outlive Ann and Larry.

"It took a long time to get here," he told Ann.

"What do you think was the most important part?" she asked.

"Always striving to do better."

38

A Question of Roots
Helsinki, Finland 1988

Of all of Ann and Larry's travels, there was one trip that held special significance to Ann. She approached Larry with the idea: "My Zonta group has a convention in Helsinki. I'd like to go."

"I thought only the president had to attend global conventions," Larry said.

"I don't have to go. But I'd like to go. I've always wanted to go to Finland—to see where Chuck Ruben Wirkkula came from." As much as she had tried, it had been difficult to completely say goodbye to the ghost of her dead husband. She hoped seeing his ancestral homeland would help her move on from him once and for all.

Ann and Larry attended Zonta's International Convention at Helsinki, Finland in 1988. They were able to meet Zonta members from around the globe.

"Was it worth the trip?" Larry asked.

"It was a wonderful convention," Ann said.

"You don't seem satisfied."

"Ever since you got me started on genealogy…Chuck's

heritage is here—both Chuck Sr. and Chuck Jr.—I want to see where they came from," Ann said.

Larry and Ann made arrangements to be chauffeured by a local married couple who spoke English. Their first stop was a Lutheran church where they found the Wirkkula genealogy. Their next destination was the settlement of Wirkkula, a farm community and place name. Discovery that the Wirkkula line was a place name, and that everyone that lived there took the name, became a stumbling block for further genealogical investigation.

They toured the farm with a man who bore a striking resemblance to Chuck Sr. For a moment, Ann felt like he had come back from the dead to accompany her through the homeland that he had never stepped foot on. They took a picture with the guide and continued their tour.

In the nearby city of Oulu they met with a woman who took them on a tour of the cemetery where several of the older Wirrkulas had been buried. Ann and Larry showed her some of the pictures they had taken of the farm.

"That's my husband!" the woman exclaimed when she saw the man. She took them to meet with the remaining Wirkkula family in Finland.

They showed Ann pictures, and Ann shared pictures that Chuck Sr.'s mother, Mrs. Wirkkula had given her. Some of the pictures were matches. She had found his family. It was a beautiful glimpse into what could have been.

However, when she looked at Larry, who eagerly made friends with these people he had no connection to, she realized that while this trip had provided her a sense of closure, her marriage to Larry had been more fulfilling than she ever could have imagined from that first meeting a few weeks before Christmas. His desire for self-improvement had been infectious, getting Ann over her shyness, encouraging her to be a prominent local business woman who always strived to do better. He had been there to stoke her competitive passions as they raced hundreds of regattas. This was the man who helped her discover where she came from, and helped her forge a legacy to hand down to her children. He was a wonderful husband and a father even if his jokes were often off-color. He was stern but loving, devoted yet demanding, and above all loyal and steadfast.

Larry had been the catalyst to grow Ann from a young woman and mother, full of ideas, into a seasoned world traveler. Together they had seen the amazing highs and lows of humanity. His grounding had been the scaffold for her ideas to flourish and grow. More than anything, she was happy with Larry. What had started as an unlikely mid-life romance had turned into lifelong companionship and love. It wasn't the red-hot love of youth, but a deeper, more complex and nuanced love. One that was greatly more nourishing to her soul. Loving Larry had made Ann complete. She smiled at him and said, "Let's go home."

39

50th Wedding Anniversary
Horton Plaza 2015

Larry adjusted the bow tie on his tuxedo. He smoothed the pencil-thin mustache that crossed his upper lip. Bald on top, his hair trimmed short on the sides—the long grey ponytail that he had sported for much of his eighties had been cut off for the occasion. He had been losing weight since his triple bypass and resulting increase in doctor prescribed exercise. The jacket of his rented tuxedo was a good fit.

In the living room, he called out, "Ann, I'm going to my office."

"Okay dear," she called from her bathroom where she was doing her makeup.

"I'll see you in the dining hall." Larry stepped from their apartment on the third floor of Horton Plaza. Outside the door was a photo of Ann smiling at Mueller Glacier on Mt Cook in New Zealand. Larry strolled the hallway, past the game room where he held the top place for their Wii Bowling season. He took the long route to the elevator as he had time and nervous energy to burn off.

Pictures and posters from their travels lined the upper

floor hallway. Chichen-Itza from the Yucatan, The Eiffel Tower in Paris, Big Ben in London, Puukoholā Heiau in Hawaii, and many more locations around the globe.

He clutched a copy of his speech for the day, but wanted to make a correction before the festivities. In his office, he booted up his computer and opened the file.

Going from poverty to the top 1%.

He deleted the line and the rest of the following paragraph. "What does it matter," he mumbled, "it doesn't matter." A moment later, his printer began ejecting pages. When done, he stapled the pages together.

He put on his reading glasses and skimmed the script for errors, reading softly to himself. "My first meeting with Ann, I took her to lunch at the Far East Chinese restaurant...wedding took place at the Episcopal Church...house to accommodate five boys...most exciting trip was in 1973 to the wedding of Craig and Jane... sailing with the local Yacht Club...one-hundred and ten trophies." He paused a moment and smiled at the memory of the trophies. They were scattered throughout his and Ann's apartment, many of them in his bathroom for lack of space to properly display them. "Ann's family dated back to Jamestown and mine to Plymouth Rock...I gave up flying a few years after having my wheels up landing at the Salem airport with Craig as my passenger."

He stopped to think about that too. It had been his first time flying in a retractable gear aircraft. He'd forgotten to put the wheels down. The propeller had been chipped and needed replacing—he had nearly died that day. And while there had been a moment after his first wife, Marty's death, that he had felt that he was no better than dead, at that darkest moment, he had met Ann. He shook the thought from his head. No. Make sure the speech was correct, he thought.

He continued to mutter words as he skimmed, "…thirty five day trip around the world…Hong Kong to Greece… we never thought we would reach our fiftieth anniversary because of health problems." Ann had her first pacemaker in 2011, just a week before a thirty-five day river boat trip up the Danube and down the Rhine. "I had heart surgery…"

Both his and Ann's parents had died. Larry and Ann had both had to cope with the death of their first spouse. Larry had lost several siblings, and Ann's brother was experiencing fading health after the death of his wife. Larry nearly lost his youngest son, Steve to disease. Together, Ann and Larry had seen much death. Larry had prepared an estate plan to continue to provide for Ann— age and gender both indicated Larry would be the first of them to go. "Death and Taxes," Larry muttered. The saying was true. Those were both unavoidable facts of life.

Larry finished his review. "All here." He tucked the script into his jacket pocket. He went to the dining room. Guests were beginning to arrive. Some of them were residents of Horton Plaza, others were friends and community figures, and most importantly to Larry, his ever growing family. Between his children, grandchildren, and great grandchildren they were nearly three-dozen and growing. He saw them each come in and reflected that this man who had come from Kansas could now boast of a family so expansive it touched the four corners of the United States.

When it became time to deliver his speech, Larry spoke from script. Many of the elements of his speech came from his earlier memoirs, some from his in-development autobiography. But they all came from Larry and Ann's shared life. Most of them anyway—he put a few business deals in and some salacious bits like his near-death landings…as he had learned from Toastmasters: use the most exciting and universal material available. He tended to keep his personal stories personal.

He wrapped his speech with, "We hope you are pleased with our families. We now have five sons, eleven grandchildren, and fourteen great grandchildren with more on the way. Thanks for being part of our fiftieth wedding anniversary."

He handed the microphone to his grandson, Larry for a toast. "When I learned you and Grandma started your relationship around the age of forty—it was a new beginning for you. This gives me hope…you have had a large hand in developing the person I am today. I could be so lucky to have half the life after forty that you have had. I love you both very much."

Larry's sons and some of the other grandchildren gave toasts. Generosity, compassion, steadfastness were common themes.

Everyone settled in for music. Ann was to sing. After her retirement, she had finally allowed herself to indulge in the arts that she had loved for her entire life. She supported Art in Bloom, purchased local art, and often sang with her son Jerry accompanying her on drums.

As Ann warmed up, Larry had a thought in the back of his mind about developing the property he had near the hospital. It was still a potential deal, one that could make another few millions that he could pass on to his family. But when he looked up, he saw Ann smiling at him as she sang *Someone to Love*.

Her gaze didn't waver from his.

Larry felt his heart catch for a moment. It didn't have to be him conquering the world. That didn't matter. Not one bit. Not with Ann singing.

Her blue eyes sparkled as her voice wavered. Emotion colored her notes. Her medley shifted to *Nearness of You*. He dabbed at the corners of his eyes to keep them dry—it was a fiftieth anniversary, he was supposed to be dignified. He watched her sing, this woman he had met in the darkest hour of his life. This woman who gave him so much light. So much to live for. Before Ann, Larry was a man of labor, of work and toil, of religious austerity and devotion. But Ann had chipped away at him for years, introducing him to the wider world.

It had been a blossoming of Larry's soul. He had gone from heartland poverty to an appreciation—no a love—for all things that life had to offer. A journey he would have never thought to undertake without Ann's cosmopolitan sensibilities. But that wasn't the entirety of it. They had both loved before. They had both had loved ripped from their hearts by death. And they had fallen together in a desperate need to love again. And they did. Their love grew and deepened as it was forged by competition on a sailboat, tempered by the exploration of their roots, adorned by their growing family.

Larry wiped again at the corner of his eyes and he watched Ann as she sang with her voice on the edge of breaking and her eyes locked on his. He watched her in this moment and he thought of nothing else. Everything he had done was to ensure their retirement. Was to ensure their family. Was to make a moment like this possible. Ann singing to Larry.

She had been his muse all these years. A muse to his investments. Investments for them. For family. She had been the muse that pulled him from darkness. The muse that showed him there was more to life than work. More to life than money. The muse that had driven him to be more than work or investment. She had unlocked his potential and had challenged him continually. She had pushed him from his comfort zone. She had consoled him when he strayed too far. She had become his life. Fifty years. Tears on the edge of his eyes. Passion on her voice. Fifty years. This is what he did it all for. Not wealth. Not success. For her. To provide for her. Nothing else mattered. This was life. This was love. This serenade. He couldn't look away from Ann. Love. Just love.

A Note on Genealogy

Larry and Ann's pursuits of their genealogical origins took them to forty-nine of the fifty United States—sorry Alabama. They were able to trace Ann's lineage to the arrival of the *Mary and Margaret* to Jamestown in 1916 as part of the historic Second Supply. Larry's earliest ancestors to reach America were Pilgrim settlers on the 1620 *Mayflower* voyage that landed at Plymouth. Their revolutionary war relatives lived less than twenty miles from each other in the then 'Rogue State' of Vermont. Their ancestors fought on both sides of the Civil War and traveled west at the behest of the Manifest Destiny. Ann's ancestors came to Oregon by covered wagon in 1852, Larry's nearly a century later. From Medford, Oregon, Larry and Ann's descendants then reversed the trend, with their grandchildren scattering across the United States, living in Washington, Oregon, California, Indiana, Michigan, New York and Florida.

Ann and Larry, 2017

Larry and Marty, circa 1946

Ann and Chuck Sr., circa 1950

Ann and Larry, 1965

Ann and Larry Racing *Peridot*

Ann and Larry, 2010

Ann and Larry, circa 1980

Ann and Larry aboard *Peridot*

Ann and Larry, 2001

Ann and Larry, 2001

Bottom Image (top left to right) Jerry, Larry, Craig (bottom left to right) Stan, Ann, Chuck, Steve.

Top Image 1965, Middle Image 1990, Bottom Image 2015

44966298R00150

Made in the USA
Middletown, DE
21 June 2017